CHARLOTTE'S CHRISTMAS CHARADE

A Sugar Plum Romance

DARCI BALOGH

Knowhere Media

For my Mom
Thank you for all of the magical Christmas holidays you worked so hard to put together. The traditions you created when I was little live on in my daughters and make our holidays joyful every year. Thank you for teaching me to love cooking, decorating and putting on a great party. Merry Christmas and Happy November Birthday Buddy, Mom!

I f there was one thing Charlotte Olsen disliked about the holidays it was traveling. She was the kind of person who liked to get settled into one place, preferably her own home, and stay there for the duration of the festivities. That's why she had avoided travel over the holidays for most of her adult life, and why she was in such a gloomy mood today, December 19th. It was just days until Christmas and she was far from home.

Charlotte clung to a section of the metal bar in the center of the packed shuttle, shoved up against other passengers, and silently fighting a throbbing headache. The subway style shuttle had picked them up on the concourse and taken them into what seemed like endless dark tunnels that snaked their way underground towards the main terminal at Denver International Airport.

Stuffed with people, the shuttle was remarkably quiet except for an old recording of *Rockin' Around the Christmas Tree* playing through the speakers. Her fellow passengers were either busy staring into their cell phones, too laden down with luggage to speak, like urban Sherpas, or staring into the middle distance with glazed expressions.

Charlotte fell into the latter category.

Her small stature meant that her view of anything besides the coat buttons, looming backs, or armpits of her fellow travelers was extremely limited. The sights and smells of public transportation were for her, at best, stuffy and, at worst, something she didn't care to think about. Combined with the stressful landing she had just endured it was no wonder she had a headache.

Her three-hour flight from Seattle had been frazzling. First it was delayed, then massive turbulence hit their plane mid flight and the whole terrifying event ended with a white knuckle landing into ice and snow. The small snowstorm they had entered somewhere over Wyoming turned into a serious winter storm in Denver while they were in the air. Charlotte was thankful to be on solid ground again, but wished she was heading to her own cozy two bedroom house instead of high up into the Rocky Mountains and even deeper into the storm.

Being on the round side of body types, she tried to take up as little space as possible to avoid bumping her behind or bosom up against her nearest neighbors. A woman next to her, wrapped in a deep brown coat with a fake fur-lined hood, carried a bulky wrapped Christmas gift that stuck out in all directions. Charlotte couldn't think what kind of gift might make a shape like that, with pieces of it wildly protruding every which way. Bagpipes? A statue of an octopus? As she pondered this question, the woman's pocket started ringing. Twisting to reach her phone, the woman shifted her wrapped gift and one of its shoots pressed into Charlotte's cheek. The wrapping was green with happy cartoon puppies, and whatever was inside the brightly colored paper was hard as steel.

"Excuse me," the woman said, focusing on Charlotte's face for the first time since they boarded the shuttle.

"No problem," Charlotte answered, trying to shift her body, and face, to give the woman some room. Before she could turn away she saw recognition register in the woman's eyes and braced herself for the inevitable question.

"Aren't you...?" The woman searched her mind for the right name. Finding it, her face lit up, "You're Chef Charlotte, aren't you?"

Her excitement caught the attention of the other passengers and they all adjusted their positions and strained to get a look at Charlotte. Charlotte cursed the fact that she hadn't tried wearing a hat over her long, dark hair to at least attempt to remain incognito.

"You are, you're Chef Charlotte," the woman continued, her tone more ecstatic than accusatory.

Charlotte put on her best patient and kind smile, expecting an onslaught of questions, comments, requests for selfies and even the occasional autograph now that she had been discovered. After her celebrity hit a little over a year ago, she had learned to keep a smile plastered on her face no matter what, otherwise someone would surely get a picture of her looking angry or ridiculous and post it all over the internet.

A murmur moved through her section of the shuttle as other passengers realized they were so close to one of America's most beloved celebrity chefs. Charlotte's smile increased the throbbing in her head, but she did not let it slip.

"I am," she admitted, ducking her head in perfectly demure acceptance.

"I love your show!" The woman had retrieved her phone, but didn't answer the call coming in. Instead she punched a few buttons and asked, "Do you mind taking a selfie with me? My sister is never going to believe this!"

3

When the shuttle finally made it to the terminal, Charlotte had fielded two-dozen questions and taken at least half that many selfies. Her head felt like it was splitting in two. She couldn't blame the fans, the show needed them after all. She could blame Bella, her assistant, who normally travelled with her and took on crowd control duties. It was Bella that should be here talking to the people. Bella was the one who had always wanted to be a star.

Unfortunately, Bella had missed their flight. Her car broke down in the middle of traffic and despite the flight's delayed take off she still hadn't made it in time. Charlotte had tried to stall the plane, but her celebrity status didn't have that kind of clout. She had called Bella as they pulled out and taxied towards the runway.

"What am I going to do?" Charlotte asked her long time friend.

"Don't panic," Bella said in her thick Spanish accent, heavier than normal because of the stress.

"When is the next flight to Denver?" Charlotte asked, panic rising in her stomach despite Bella's suggestion.

"I don't know, but I'll find one. Everything will be fine."

Charlotte didn't know about that. When she wasn't tightly gripping her armrests during the turbulence on her flight, she wracked her brain trying to think of different scenarios where Bella not arriving at their Christmas destination would be fine. She couldn't think of one.

Charlotte and Bella had worked side-by-side, practically inseparable, on the cable TV sensation cooking show, Chef Charlotte's Kitchen, since its inception. They had been friends since college, auditioned for the celebrity chef position as a team, and were connected at the hip because of the show, and because they were best friends.

In fact, you could say Chef Charlotte was nothing without Bella and you wouldn't be far from the truth. While Charlotte was a cute, blue-eyed brunette with photogenic skin the color of cream, who also possessed a particular knack for quick-witted responses and a flair for style and decorating, she had one fatal void in her talents as a celebrity chef. Charlotte could not cook. Not the No Culinary Art Degree kind of not being able to cook, but the Burn Everything/Can't Boil Water/Disaster in a Kitchen kind.

The shuttle doors opened and Charlotte made her way with her new group of doting fans down the corridor towards the escalators. She took a brief moment to break away from their attentions and look down at her phone.

One long text from Bella.

I have an idea. I packed a dozen pastries in your carry-on in case of emergency. This is an emergency! Give them those for breakfast. Make some coffee. I will be there by then. Call me when you land.

This was a disaster. Although, Charlotte did make a decent cup of coffee. That was the one and only thing she could do in the kitchen.

She stepped onto the escalator, carefully placing her rolling carry-on next to her feet. Her spirits lifted slightly, knowing that she had breakfast in the bag, so to speak. Pastries and coffee. She could do that.

Charlotte hadn't set out to be a fraud. She and Bella met in college and became fast friends. Charlotte studied interior design and Bella went for a culinary arts degree. Bella was an intuitive and exciting chef and she convinced Charlotte to audition with her for a new cooking show. Bella would be the chef and Charlotte would be her witty assistant who could plate and present the food with panache.

Nothing had turned out how they planned.

On the day of their audition, Bella had come down with a horrible stomach flu. She didn't want to touch the food and make the judges sick, she could barely look at food without throwing up. Instead of give up their audition slot, the two friends decided to switch places just for the day, with Bella whispering instructions to Charlotte. Their plan worked. Everyone loved them...well, they loved Charlotte. They offered Charlotte the job and in what she now looked back on as a fit of insanity, she and Bella decided to team up together on a very big secret. Charlotte accepted the job on the condition that Bella was hired as her assistant.

Nobody knew that Bella was the real cooking talent behind the show, not the producers, not the crew, nobody. Their charade had worked well, so well that Chef Charlotte's Kitchen blew up to the top cable TV cooking show within six months of its first episode airing. Neither she nor Bella had ever expected her to reach the kind of fame and success she had so quickly attained. So far, they had managed the ruse and kept their secret from the world with virtually no hiccups. Until now.

Charlotte stepped off the escalator and walked through the tall glass doors into Denver's main terminal. Giant tinsel decorations in the form of Santa and his reindeers hung from the huge white peaked ceiling, as if they were swooshing over the holiday travelers below. Tall, thin Christmas trees lined the center of the terminal, blinking bright white lights that showed off decorations in hot pink and Grinch green. Throngs of friends and family waited just on the other side of a roped off walkway. *It's the Most Wonderful Time of the Year* rang through the air, mixing with the sounds of talking and laughing as people were reunited with loved ones.

Charlotte kept her smile in place, even though her cheeks were aching from the effort. She walked briskly along the roped off area looking for her ride. Not a friend or family member, but a chauffeur. A driver from the Crystal Lake Inn where she was expected to cook for the owners and their VIP guests over the Christmas holiday. Anxious thoughts invaded her mind. Cooking Christmas dinner without Bella? Her palms started sweating at the idea.

"Miss Olsen? Charlotte Olsen?" A deep voice called out to her from inside in the crowd. She saw a man's hand lift a sign with her name written on it above the crowd, waving it back and forth.

"Yes," she stopped and waited as a tall man with white hair and bushy white eyebrows emerged from the wall of people.

He was over 60, with a large nose and a face that looked creased from too many years squinting into the sun and wind. In one hand he held the sign, in the other, a beat up, black cowboy hat.

"I'm Bill, Bill Logan. Davis sent me to get you," he stuck out a large hand that Charlotte took cordially. Bill glanced behind her, "I thought there were two of you."

If only.

"No, my assistant missed the flight, unfortunately. She'll be joining us in the morning."

"Well, I don't know about that. It's really coming down out there," Bill scratched his head and looked worried.

Charlotte's stomach sank.

Sensing her worry, he smiled at her and put on his hat. Then, reaching for her carry on he said, "We better get a move on to get back up the mountain. We'll do what we can in the morning to get your assistant..." he gave her a questioning look, wanting her to fill in the blank.

"Bella, her name's Bella," Charlotte answered, focusing hard on being as professional as possible.

Bill nodded, "We'll do what we can to get Bella up the mountain tomorrow."

Charlotte smiled as if that was the best plan she'd ever heard, but inside her nerves were in melt down.

CHAPTER 2

S nuggled into the front seat of a full sized pickup, Charlotte was warm and cozy, but confused. Was this giant old pickup the transportation Crystal Lake Inn sent for all their guests? Not quite the normal resort experience.

"Are you sure you don't want to put your bag in the back?" Bill asked, eyeing the carry on Charlotte had insisted they squeeze in between them on the bench seat. "I can tarp it like I did your big suitcase."

"No," Charlotte tried to look less squished on her side of the seat. "Thank you, I'd rather keep it inside to be safe," she placed her hand on the bag to emphasize her decision. "My laptop's in here," she explained, though she was more worried about the pastries.

They drove out of the parking garage into thick clouds and heavy snow. There was no hint of the famous bright blue skies of Colorado, just an endless grey and what looked like a growing blanket of white over everything. As they started up the icy highway, Charlotte was comforted by the steady strength of the pickup carrying them.

She peered out the windshield to look at the snow swirling down, "Is this supposed to stop any time soon?"

"Nope, it's supposed to come down pretty hard. Harder than anyone thought it would," Bill answered. He looked sideways at her and added, "Just in time for Christmas." Then he turned up the radio on the dash, "Want some music?" He asked as *Feliz Navidad* filled the cab.

Charlotte nodded politely and they fell into silence, Bill because he was driving and Charlotte because she was staring out the window watching the winter storm. The rumbling of the big pickup combined with fatigue from her flight and the mesmerizing view of falling snow, and before she could stop herself Charlotte fell asleep.

She woke up to a cheerful, if staticky, country rendition of *Winter Wonderland* playing on the radio and nothing but darkness outside her window. She sat forward with a start, not remembering where she was for a moment. Bill spoke to her while keeping his eyes on the road ahead.

"We're off the highway now. Might be another half hour to get to the Inn with the roads this bad," he informed her.

Charlotte cleared the sleep from her throat, "Okay, how long have I been asleep?"

Bill chuckled, "Almost two hours, you missed out on all the traffic coming up I-70."

"Two hours?" Charlotte was surprised, but not completely, "I get tired when I'm stressed."

"Oh, don't you worry about the roads. We've got it handled," he patted the dashboard of the pickup like it was an old friend.

Charlotte peered out the windshield where huge snowflakes appeared in the beams from the headlights and barreled towards them, splatting against the glass where they were immediately swept away by two long windshield wipers. She could barely see the road for all of the snow, but what she could see didn't look like a road at all. It looked more like they were driving straight through drifts of snow, some of them almost as high as the headlights themselves.

"You can see the road in this?" She asked.

"I know the road, I don't need to see it," Bill responded with a quick, reassuring wink.

Charlotte was only mildly reassured. As the pickup carried them presumably further and further into the middle of nowhere, she pondered the odds of them ending up stranded in a blizzard. If the roads were this bad now, how would Bella ever make it up here in the morning? Charlotte's brows pinched together with worry. Maybe it would be better to be stranded and freezing than have to face cooking for a room full of strangers who were expecting Chef Charlotte.

"There it is," Bill informed her, pointing at a tiny glowing orb in the distance.

"What is that?" Charlotte asked, leaning forward as far as her seatbelt would allow.

"That's the yard light at the Inn. We'll be there real soon, not to worry," Bill explained.

So much for escaping her fate by getting stranded in a blizzard.

As they approached, the glowing orb grew bigger and bigger and other smaller orbs appeared hanging lower towards the ground.

"Here we go," Bill announced, slowing the pickup.

Suddenly they were close enough to the light to see through the heavy snow and she could make out a wide drive with a wooden fence running along both sides. The orbs became clearer and she could see one was a yard light at the top of a telephone pole, one was a light on what appeared to be the wide doors of a red barn, and one was a porch light hung next to a large, white building with a door painted bright red and hung with a wreath.

Charlotte gasped as the scene became clear, thousands of little white lights wrapped around the fence in front of the house and hung around the windows and along the eaves high on the two-story building. There were also white lights making up an oversized wreath shape above the doors of the barn. The lights shone bravely through the haze of the storm, the snow fell in fat flakes, and there was a hint of tall pine trees surrounding the house and barn.

"It's beautiful," she sighed. She was overcome momentarily with the sight of the place, enough to forget her current dilemma, briefly.

Bill pulled the pickup close to the red front door and put it in park, but left it running. He leaned forward and looked up at the Inn with the lights and the snow, and agreed.

"That it is, Miss Olsen."

"Oh, please," Charlotte said, "Call me Charlotte."

"Not Chef Charlotte?" He asked with a grin.

She shook her head, "No, please, that's absolutely unnecessary."

"All right, Charlotte, hang tight a minute and we'll get you inside safe and sound."

She watched as Bill got out of the pickup and trudged around the front through the light of the headlamps, disappearing into the red door. The snow piled up quickly on the hood of the pickup as she watched and waited. Another Christmas carol, *Here Comes Santa Claus*, played on the radio. She wished she could enjoy this experience more, it certainly looked like a beautiful place. Bella had been right about that.

Bella! She hadn't called her when she landed. Charlotte pulled out her cell phone and hit Bella's button. She answered on the first ring.

"Charlie! I've been worried!" Bella's greeting was loud and fretting.

"I'm here, sorry I didn't call you. The flight was crazy then I fell asleep on the way up here."

"You're sleeping?"

"No, I slept during the ride into the mountains. I'm at the Inn now." Charlotte looked up into the yard light where it seemed as if the giant snowflakes were falling thicker and faster than before, "It's really snowing hard. Please tell me you got a flight in tonight instead of tomorrow."

"The flights have all been cancelled," Bella told her.

"What?" Charlotte's anxiety returned ten fold.

"The storm is bad in Denver and they won't let anybody land," Bella explained.

Charlotte dropped her head into her hand and closed her eyes. She thought she might throw up.

"It's okay, it's going to be okay," Bella tried to reassure her.

"How is it going to be okay? I'm here! There are people expecting me to cook for them!" Charlotte argued, rubbing her eyes with her fingertips, trying to erase the knowledge Bella had just shared.

"I'm going to drive there," Bella told her.

"Drive? It's a two day drive to Denver! I can't be alone with these people for two days."

Just then, the driver's door opened and cold air rushed into the cab. Charlotte looked up, startled at the interruption. It wasn't Bill, but a much younger man wearing a bulky, unbuttoned coat over a blue plaid flannel shirt. He leaned over the seat reaching for her carry on.

"Hi," he said, his big, blue eyes smiling at her. His hair was a messy tumble of thick, dark curls topped off with fat snowflakes, as he wasn't wearing a hat. He had a larger nose, like Bill's, and a kind face. She wondered if they were related somehow. She could see Bill retrieving her big suitcase from under the tarp in the back of the pickup. Maybe this was his son.

"Hi," Charlotte answered.

"What are you saying?" Bella asked, her voice carrying out of the speaker and through the cab. Charlotte smiled apologetically at Bill's son. She pointed at her cell phone and mouthed the word 'sorry'. He nodded in understanding, pulled her carry on out of the cab and closed the door.

Charlotte spoke again, keeping her voice low, "I cannot be alone up here for two days, Bella. Two whole days of meals?"

"I know, Charlie, I know," Bella sounded as upset as Charlotte felt.

They shared a few quiet moments of despair.

"You have the pastries, right?" Bella asked.

Charlotte watched Bill's son follow Bill into the red door, holding her carry on, "Yes."

"Let me think of what to do. There must be another airport in Colorado. I'll call you back."

Charlotte sighed, "Okay."

There was nothing left to do but go inside and somehow keep everyone in the Inn from thinking, or talking about, or needing to eat food until Bella got here. Not likely.

Charlotte climbed out of the pickup into the snow. She didn't have a hat either and she could see soft flakes sticking to her hair where it fell halfway down her chest. She left the pickup still chugging in park behind her and walked to the red door.

The Crystal Lake Inn was bigger than she'd expected. Painted white with black shutters on each tall window, of which it looked like there were thirteen total, three on either side of the red door and seven evenly spaced along the second story. Under the fresh pine wreath on the door there was an ornate iron knocker and she saw a historical marker plaque nailed to the right of the door.

Charlotte pushed the door open and stepped into a foyer with high ceilings and several rag rugs tossed haphazardly around, covering the floors. A flurry of cold air and wet snow followed her in and Bill's son, who was stamping snow off his unlaced boots, looked up at the commotion.

"Sorry," Charlotte said as she closed the door behind her.

He dismissed her apology with a wave and said, "You can hang your coat here to dry." Charlotte glanced at the row of thick wooden pegs sticking out of the wall, then around the rest of the foyer. No luggage to be seen.

"My bags?" She asked.

"They're in your room, upstairs."

"Thank you."

Bill's son kicked his boots off completely, placing them carefully next to three other pairs of boots lined up along a section of the wall where a radiator emanated heat. His coat was already hung on one of the wooden pegs and when he stood in front of her, about 6'2" in stocking feet, she was a little surprised at his casual demeanor. His worn jeans had splashes of mud up the legs and he wore a floppy blue T-shirt underneath his blue plaid flannel. With a five-o-clock shadow and tumbled, out of control locks, he definitely had a playful charm about him, but he didn't look like any hotel or Inn worker she'd ever encountered. They certainly were informal here at Crystal Lake.

He looked her up and down with an amused expression, like he was expecting her to say something funny, "So, you're the Chef Charlotte everyone's been talking about."

"Yes," Charlotte gave him a tolerant smile, "That's me."

"What do you think of the Inn?"

She flicked her gaze around the foyer then back to Bill's son, giving him a 'meh' face, "It's definitely...rustic."

He caught the dig with grace, tossing his head back a little as he let out a laugh. Then he rested his hands on his hips and chuckled in self deprecating style, "That's exactly what my

15

wife, excuse me, my ex-wife used to say about it." He stuck out his hand, "Davis Reed."

Charlotte placed her hand in his just as his name registered. Her eyebrows raised in surprise, "Mr. Reed? The owner?"

"Yep, lucky me," he shook her hand warmly, then dropped it and turned to leave the foyer. "Follow me, Miss Olsen. I'll show you to your room."

He led her through a large, warm living room where a fire crackled in a stone fireplace and worn, brown leather couches seemed a comfortable place to sit, if not spectacular to look at. They continued down a narrow hallway where they had to walk single file.

"The kitchen is that way," Davis indicated an open door to a dark room. "We've already eaten, so no need to worry about any of that tonight. Just chili. We eat a lot of chili. I make a mean batch of chili if I do say so myself, won an award for it at the chili fair a few years ago," he looked back at her with a grin. "I expect we won't have anything that rustic while you're here."

"Ha," Charlotte pretended to think he was funny.

"Bill told me about your assistant missing the plane. It doesn't look like any more flights are coming in for a while with this storm."

"Yes," Charlotte said miserably.

They started up a stairway with a beautifully carved antique wood handrail.

"I guess it's a good thing you didn't miss the plane or we would be in a world of hurt," he said

Charlotte's stomach twisted into a knot.

Davis Reed stopped at the top of the stairs and motioned her towards a door to their right. The door was painted robin's egg blue with a black iron '3' hanging on the front.

"This is you," he said.

The room was beautiful. Small, but beautiful. A deep blue rug with flecks of gold covered most of the hardwood floors. An elaborately designed antique iron headboard stood, elegant, against the cool white walls. There was a luxurious white down comforter and several white lace pillows covering the bed along with a pale blue fuzzy blanket draped across the foot.

Charlotte took in the lovely decor, but was having a difficult time focusing on anything except her own terrible problem.

"It's not our biggest room, I had to save that for the guests you're here to impress," Davis said.

"Mr. Reed, without my assistant—" Charlotte began, maybe she could talk him down from his expectations.

"Don't you worry about that. We got everything on the list you emailed, so you have all of the supplies you need." He put his hands on either side of the doorframe and leaned into her room, eager to tell her his thoughts, "And I can chop vegetables and wash pots and pans to help you out. Whatever you need, Miss Olsen, just ask."

"Call me Charlotte," she told him with a quiet sigh. Her mind was running away with all of the possible doom and gloom situations this holiday was going to bring.

He grinned at her, "And you call me Davis." He paused for a moment, noticing the concern on her face, "It's just me and Bill here until the Foss' and their guests arrive, which hopefully will be tomorrow sometime. If they can make the trip with this snow. Anyway, you don't have to worry about doing anything impressive in the kitchen just for us. Wait until the Foss' and the Biddlebumps to pull out your big chef guns."

The strange name threw her out of her thoughts. She'd been so busy worrying she hadn't been paying close attention to what he said. Charlotte tilted her head and asked, "Sorry, who?"

"Dennis and Victoria Foss are possible investors who may want to partner with me on the Inn. And they invited their good friends, the Biddlebumps, to spend the holiday here," he explained.

The corner of Charlotte's mouth twitched into a smile, "The Biddlebumps?"

Davis lifted one shoulder and let it drop in a loose shrug, "I know. But they're special friends of the Foss' I guess, so we're gonna try to impress all of them with your cooking."

Her temporary amusement faded. No matter how silly their names were, they were two more mouths to feed. Not just feed, she was expected to impress these people—rich people. She was doomed, and trapped, and a fraud, and a failure. As soon as Davis left, she flopped onto the iron bed and cried until she fell into a dismal sleep.

CHAPTER 3

C harlotte woke in the morning to a chilly room. The old Inn had a particular charm in the daylight, but she practically shivered from the cold as she went to her window to check out the weather.

"Oh no," Charlotte muttered under her breath after opening the deep blue curtains. She stared out over the front drive. The tall yard light and red barn she recognized from the night before, but just barely, because the snow was still coming down and every flat, or almost flat, surface was covered with a pile of the white stuff that looked to be at least three feet high. If Charlotte wasn't so miserable, she may have found being snowed in at this place rather magical. Not today, however, today was not going to be a magical day.

Checking her phone she saw that she had no messages from Bella at all. She tried to call her, but the call failed and Charlotte realized she had no bars, no cell service. Maybe she could get service outside, like she had the night before in the pickup.

She got ready quickly, bumping around in the pretty, but very small, bathroom. She managed to prepare for the day in record time. She wanted to get downstairs and make coffee as soon as possible. The smell of freshly brewed coffee usually put everyone in a good mood. With that and the pastries on the table she could buy enough time to hop outside and try to reach Bella and see what her friend had planned.

Opening her carry-on she pulled out two white boxes tied up with red ribbon that came from an excellent bakery in Seattle. One box held strawberries and cream rolled pastries, and the other was full of apple turnovers. Thank goodness Bella had thought ahead. She really hoped her friend came up with an idea on how to save more than just breakfast.

Walking into the kitchen, Charlotte was taken aback by its ample size. With floor to ceiling wood cabinets and creamy stone counter tops it had a real old-time feel. Though traditional in style, it obviously contained everything necessary to cook for large crowds, including a six-burner gas stove and a catering style, double door stainless steel refrigerator. There was a wide island down the center of the room, with cabinets underneath and a small sink set into one side. Along the outside wall there were two tall windows overlooking the back yard and a long wood plank table with eight high backed chairs tucked neatly against it.

Luckily there was no sign of Davis or Bill, so Charlotte got to work.

She located the coffee pot and searched through the cupboards for coffee. She came across some beautiful stoneware and other table decorations before finding the ground coffee and took what she liked for the morning presentation. She put the coffee on to brew, then chose some red dessert plates and white cloth napkins, arranging them artfully at one end of the table. Laying the pastries out on two napkins that she had placed in a low serving dish, she lifted the edges of the napkins up and over the pastries, tying the top closed with one of the red ribbons from the boxes.

She cut the other ribbon in half and used it to tie pretty bows on the handles of the creamer and sugar bowl, which she made sure to fill.

When she was done the simple breakfast looked like a photo shoot and the smell of fresh coffee filled the room. Pleased, Charlotte grabbed her cell phone and headed to the foyer to retrieve her jacket and go outside to call Bella.

The snow was still coming down, and she was afraid there wasn't much cover outside. Spying a few umbrellas leaning in the corner by the radiator, Charlotte picked one and opened it as she stepped out the door. She gasped when the cold hit her face and her breath hung in the air when she exhaled. She checked her phone, one bar. She took a few steps into the driveway, two bars. About fifteen feet out, which was smack dab in the middle of the driveway, she had three bars, enough to make a call.

"Tell me you have a plan," she said when Bella answered.

"I'm in my car right now," Bella said.

Charlotte's hopes sank, "You're driving?"

The front door opened and Charlotte whirled towards the noise. Davis stood in the doorway looking out at her with his brows knit in concern, squinting through the snowflakes.

"Is everything okay?" He asked.

"Yes!" Charlotte answered a little too loud and cheery, "Everything's fine. I'm just..." she couldn't make up a story fast enough. Her mind froze. Why would anyone be outside in the freezing cold? In her panic she jumped on the first reason she could think of, "Just a nicotine fit. Gotta get that morning puff!" She turned slightly so it was possible she could be holding a cigarette at her side and he couldn't see it. She looked away from him, held her empty fingers to her mouth and pretended to suck in, then blew out making what she hoped looked like a cloud of cigarette smoke in the cold morning air.

She turned back to him and smiled wide. Davis' smile was a little uncertain, but he stepped back and started to close the door.

"There's a little breakfast for you and Bill in the kitchen," Charlotte added in a high pitched, musical tone. She didn't want him to think she'd been up to nothing except smoking all morning. She had been hired as the chef after all.

He lifted his hand in acknowledgement and shut the door. Charlotte turned immediately away so her voice wouldn't carry to the house.

"You're driving?" She hissed into the phone, "You're never going to get here!"

"There are no flights at all, Charlie. I'm sorry."

Charlotte thought she might cry and wondered for a moment if the tears would freeze to her numb cheeks.

"What am I going to do, Bella?" She whimpered, "How am I going to fool them?"

"I will talk you through it," Bella offered. "First thing you need to do is tell me what you have to work with."

"The owner says they got everything on our list," Charlotte told her.

"Good! Very good," Bella was enthusiastic.

"Only if you had frozen pizzas on the list," Charlotte replied. That was her black humor rearing its ugly head under stress.

"I will help you over the phone. I need to know what they have in cans or frozen. Just read it off to me."

"I can't, I'm not in the kitchen. I'm outside."

"What are you doing outside? Aren't you in a blizzard?"

"I really needed a smoke. It helps with my anxiety," Charlotte said darkly.

"What?"

"Never mind."

"Can you go inside and make a list then call me? Hope-

22

fully I can work out something for lunch with canned goods. That would be easiest."

Charlotte agreed, though she didn't think any of this was going to be easy. Why hadn't she paid closer attention when she was fake cooking on her show and retained some of the cooking tips? It had all been such a blur and Bella was always there ready to hand her something or fix whatever she did wrong on camera. Now she was alone. And freezing.

Charlotte rubbed her hands together and blew on them to try to warm them up as she walked back to the kitchen. When she got there, she saw Davis and Bill sitting at the table munching on pastries. Bill lifted his coffee mug to her in a toast.

"There she is! Thank you, Charlotte, this is a good cup of Joe," Bill said.

She gave them a humble smile, "Oh, they're just a little treat from a bakery back home." She stopped at the coffee pot and poured herself a cup before joining them at the table.

"These are good, this is my third," Davis agreed, holding up a half eaten strawberries and cream pastry and taking a big bite.

"I'm glad you like them," she answered, adding cream and sugar to her coffee. She looked appreciatively around the kitchen, "This is a beautiful kitchen. Did you remodel it?"

Davis finished swallowing before he answered, "Yes, we did. Well, I helped my parents. I was in high school." He looked at Bill for confirmation. Bill munched on an apple turnover, giving a grunt and a nod in agreement.

"This was your parent's place?"

"Yep, and my grandparents. My great grandparents built it," His gaze traveled lovingly across the room as he spoke.

Charlotte raised her eyebrows, impressed, "Really?" She took another look at the large, beautiful kitchen, her eyes running along the woodwork and window frames, "That's really something, it's gorgeous."

Davis nodded, pleased at her appreciation. The pride he felt about his family history showed on his face.

"Was it always an Inn?" She asked, taking a sip of her coffee.

Bill grunted into his cup while Davis looked down at the table, fidgeting with his. What might be considered a blush reddened his cheeks for a moment. He cocked his head and answered without looking up.

"No, it started as a small cattle ranch. Then it was just my parent's home. We opened it as an Inn about five years ago."

Bill looked at Charlotte from underneath his wild, white eyebrows, "She changed it to an Inn."

"My ex-wife was the driving force behind it," Davis explained, half confessing. Bill snorted. Davis gave him a patient smile. "She thought it could be a big success so we sunk money into remodeling the bedrooms and adding some bathrooms, redoing the plumbing and electricity, getting permits and licenses," he let out a little sigh, remembering the money spent. She couldn't blame him, it must have cost a small fortune. "But it didn't work out like she thought it would. None of it worked out."

Charlotte nodded in understanding. It was too bad, the Inn really was charming, as was Davis. He struck her as one of those nice husbands that will do whatever his wife wants in order to keep her happy. Not a bad quality in a man, unless he ends up with the wrong kind of wife.

"But, all of that is in the past," Davis gathered himself, deciding to be optimistic. He sat up straight and gave her a hopeful smile. "This week is gonna turn the luck of the Crystal Lake Inn around. We've got tons of snow," he used his coffee cup to gesture towards the snowy scene outside the window. Then he shifted and lifted his cup to Bill, "We've got

Bill here, our captain of team driving, ready to take everyone on bonafide Christmas sleigh rides."

Charlotte was delighted at that idea, "Sleigh rides? How fun!"

"Yep," Davis' smile reached his eyes and she felt a jolt of pleasure as he focused his attention on her alone, "If it ever stops snowing you will be the first to go on a sleigh ride."

She couldn't help but laugh.

"And finally," Davis lifted his coffee cup to her, looking at her with warm, unassuming eyes, "we have you, Charlotte, to impress everyone, especially Dennis and Victoria Foss. And if they're impressed enough by their experience here, maybe they'll invest their money and the Inn can get out of the red!"

"Here's hoping," Bill said.

Bill lifted his mug to clink Davis', and Charlotte did the same. She kept a confident smile stuck to her face the whole time, though his words sent a stab of guilt straight through her chest.

CHAPTER 4

C harlotte spent the rest of the morning attempting to act calm and collected while Davis or Bill were nearby. About mid-morning they went out to the barn to tend to the horses and get the sleigh ready for use. As soon as they weren't around, Charlotte began hurrying frantically between the kitchen and her chosen 'smoking section' outside to convene in secret with Bella on the phone.

"Give it to me," Bella said when Charlotte told her she'd made a list of the available canned goods.

"Corn, green beans, chili, diced tomatoes, diced green chilies, chicken noodle soup, tomato soup, peas, boxes of cornbread and blueberry muffin mix, saltine crackers, cheese nip crackers, pinto beans, kidney beans, and Spam," Charlotte read off the list she'd jotted down on a small pad of paper next to the microwave.

"Okay, great!"

"Great?" Charlotte did not share her friend's enthusiasm.

"You can make toast, right?" Bella asked.

Charlotte hesitated.

Bella scolded, "You can at least make toast, can't you?"

"Sure," Charlotte wasn't sure of anything right now, standing in the freezing cold with snow tumbling down over her umbrella, pretending to smoke a cigarette so that her real reason for being outside would remain secret. She was tired of having secrets.

"Charlie, you're going to have to focus," Bella's voice was like a drill sergeant, snapping Charlotte out of her funk. "I know you're scared, but you can do this. I'm going to spell it out for you step by step."

Bella instructed her to go inside and find a two quart saucepan, dump two cans of tomato soup and one can of the diced tomatoes into it, then put it on low and call her back. Charlotte did as she was told. She was back outside calling Bella in a few, short minutes.

"Okay, now, I'm going to tell you how to make grilled cheese sandwiches," Bella told her.

Charlotte's stomach twisted with dismay. She was terrible with gas stoves and frying pans and flammable things like oil and butter. But she remained determined and followed Bella's instructions exactly, going outside to check with her on the phone as needed, which was often, and running into Davis several times somewhere along the way. He was back inside the house taking care of Innkeeper tasks, whatever those were, and there was nothing she could do to avoid him.

Each time they passed he smiled and nodded, but after a while his smile was just a polite facade that thinly veiled his growing puzzlement. She dealt with it by seeming extremely busy, like she didn't have a moment to spare to stop and talk or answer any questions. He didn't say anything to her, just ducked out of her way when he saw her coming and watched her disappear either back into the kitchen or out the front door.

When lunch was ready, Charlotte was relatively confident it

would taste okay. Following Bella's strict instructions, she'd added a quarter cup of cream, some fresh basil that had been special purchased for their visit, and sea salt to the doctored tomato soup. She'd also managed grilled cheese without turning on the stove by toasting the bread first then putting slices of cheese in between and melting them in the microwave.

Serving was where Charlotte's abilities finally came into play. She found turquoise blue bowls and combined them with white plates. She cut the grilled cheese into triangles and placed the triangles along with a steaming blue bowl full of tomato soup onto each plate. She added saltine and cheese nip crackers displayed nicely on a larger turquoise plate in the center of the table for fun and stepped back. It was no grand buffet, but it would work for a simple lunch.

"You have quite the habit, don't you?" Davis' voice startled her from the kitchen doorway. She turned to see him leaning against the door jam.

"What do you mean?"

Davis lifted two fingers to his mouth and flipped them back and forth, miming cigarette smoking.

"Oh, right. Yeah, I guess. Nerves," she responded.

"Nerves," Davis said, but in a way that suggested he didn't quite believe her reason. "Well, thanks for keeping the smoking outside of the Inn. We do advertise as non-smoking."

"Sure, I understand," Charlotte answered. She gestured towards the table where the steaming hot soup and sandwiches waited, "Lunch?"

They sat down together at the table. Davis explained that Bill had taken his pickup to do some plowing of the drive and would be back soon. Charlotte waited nervously for Davis to take his first spoonful of soup so she could watch his reaction. He took a bite and swallowed.

"Mmm," he said, taking another bite before saying, "That's good. You made this from plain tomato soup?"

Charlotte nodded. Happy that he liked it, but afraid he didn't like the fact she'd used regular old canned tomato soup.

"I'll have to get the recipe," he said as he looked appreciatively at the table settings she'd put together. "I have a question for you," he continued, picking up a grilled cheese triangle and dipping it into his soup before taking a bite.

"Yes?" Charlotte answered, stirring her own soup to cool it off, but also because she didn't think she could eat a thing with the nerves in her belly going wacko.

"You're really good at this," Davis swirled his half eaten grilled cheese in a circle over their lunch.

She shrugged to deflect the compliment. She didn't deserve it.

"I mean, not just the food, which is great, but all of it," he popped the rest of his grilled cheese into his mouth and chewed happily, spreading his hands out towards the table setting.

"Oh, the setting? Well, you have some really nice dishes and tableware," she tried to return the compliment.

Davis chewed and nodded and Charlotte was charmed at his enthusiasm. He seemed like a nice guy, and his tousled, super casual good looks made it even easier to like him. He swallowed and wiped his mouth on the turquoise and orange napkins she'd found in a linen drawer.

"Would you be willing to help me with some of the decorating?" He asked, "I know it's not part of the agreement and you're short handed and everything." His shoulders slumped a little in defeat and he gave her a sheepish look, "It's just there's all these boxes of my Mom's and my Grandma's full of Christmas stuff and Christmas dishes and I don't have any idea how to make it look good, if any of it can look good."

Charlotte's heart lifted a little bit at the idea. She would rather decorate this beautiful old Inn with Christmas antiques than spend one more minute cooking in the kitchen.

Davis reached out and touched her forearm, the warmth of his fingertips tingled on her skin, "Not anything big. We're going to cut a Christmas tree tomorrow and get that set up, and the lights I can handle, they're mostly all hung anyway. I'm just at a loss at what to do with any of the other stuff."

"I love decorating," Charlotte admitted, tickled at the idea of trimming a fresh cut Christmas tree.

If the chance to decorate instead of cook wasn't enough to make Charlotte happy, Davis' reaction was. Delight and relief spread over his face as an ear-to-ear smile that was so wide and appealing she couldn't help but return it with one of her own. His blue eyes twinkled at her and she suddenly felt like she might be able to do some good while she was here, instead of only ruining the food.

"The boxes are in the living room. Do you want to go through them after lunch?" He looked at her hopefully, then with uncertainty, "Unless you won't have time."

She answered immediately, "After lunch would be perfect."

Two hours later they were immersed in a sea of cardboard boxes, packing paper and Christmas decor from the past fifty years. Settled comfortably on the leather sofa in front of the fire while the snow fell outside, Davis took Charlotte on a trip down his family's Christmas memory lane.

They found vintage glass tree ornaments carefully stored in the original boxes. Davis told her how he and his brother were never allowed to touch the ornaments and he thought there were probably years that his Mom never even took them out of their boxes for fear her sons would break one. Charlotte fell in love with two-dozen bottlebrush Christmas trees of all different colors and sizes. Davis explained his Dad had found at an estate sale and bought them for his Mother one year. Davis was delighted when she pulled four hand knit, stretched out Christmas stockings from one of the boxes.

"Those were our stockings!" He laughed, admiring them with almost childlike joy, "My Mom made them. Oh, man, they're awful aren't they?"

Charlotte laughed, "No, they're not awful. They're hand-made by your Mom, that makes them perfect."

"She used to knit all the time," he smiled at the memory. "I have a Christmas sweater she made one year. It's just terrible," he chuckled to himself.

"I bet it's adorable," she said.

"How about these?" Davis asked. He held up two large plastic Santas that were about two feet tall.

"What are those?" Charlotte asked, laughing at their campy look.

Davis cocked his brow at her and cleared his throat like he was making a grand announcement, "These are part of my Dad's glowing Santa Claus collection."

They both laughed this time. Davis sat back and looked out over all of the boxes. He sighed with good natured resolve, "There's nothing we can use, is there?" He looked at her, "I'm sorry I wasted your time."

Charlotte shook her head in denial, "No, that's not true. You didn't waste my time."

"You want to use some of this?" He waved his arm towards the mess of packing material and decorations.

"I do! There's some really great Christmas china there," she pointed at three boxes she'd set aside on the coffee table. "And there are tons of these vintage bulbs," she held up an unopened package of large, multi-colored bulbs, "do you need these for the lights?"

"Nope, those were extras my Dad always bought and never used. Haven't used those lights in decades."

"I might be able to use them. And..." she grinned at

Davis, shifting her eyes to the box in front of him, "I kind of love the glowing Santas."

He laughed out loud, "No you don't!"

"I do!"

"You do?" He held up one of the smaller Santas who was molded into a cowboy style, riding a plastic reindeer, "You're crazy."

"Seriously, I think I can set up something cute with them."

Charlotte pulled the box closer to her and rummaged through it looking at all of the sizes and styles of gaudy plastic Santas. She thought she might group them all together in the foyer with some white lights and it would be a fun, casual way to greet anyone entering the Inn.

"You must really like decorating," Davis observed.

She paused and looked up at him, wondering, "Why do you say that?"

"You haven't taken a smoke break in, like, three hours."

Charlotte wrinkled her brow, forgetting that she was a fake smoker now in addition to being a fake chef.

"Oh, right," she remembered. She wiggled her head and rolled her eyes in an exaggerated 'silly me' way, "My smoking!" The pleasantness of the last few hours drained quickly away as she remembered that dinner was fast approaching. Since it had taken her over two hours to make canned soup and microwave grilled cheese sandwiches, she should probably call Bella for help preparing the evening meal.

Just then, Bill entered.

"I've got good news and bad news," he told them.

"What's the good news?" Davis asked.

"Looks like the snow is letting up."

Davis and Charlotte turned towards the window. It was still snowing, but it was easy to see that it was not coming down nearly as hard as it had been earlier. Joy surged through

Charlotte. Surely if the storm was ending Bella could get here sooner rather than later and everything would be fine. She glanced at Davis relaxing on the couch next to her, his arm thrown casually across the back so that it almost felt like she belonged there with him. Everything might turn out more than fine, actually.

"What's the bad news, then?" Davis asked.

"The roads are closed everywhere. The passes are closed. There's been about five feet of snow here, but in other areas they got over seven. Roads are gonna be a mess for days," Bill answered, unaware that he was crushing Charlotte's hopes with every word.

Davis took the information in stride. He shifted his attention back to her, "Looks like you're off the hook."

She swallowed hard, "What do you mean?"

"Well, if the Foss' and the Biddlebumps can't get here, there's nobody to cook for," he answered.

"Right..." the relief she felt at this statement was countered only by her concern over his investors not showing up. She wondered how much he was really counting on them.

"You know what?" Davis said, sitting up and putting his hand on her knee. His touch sent a zing through her stomach. "Since we've got all this out, why don't I help you put up some of the things you like and we heat up some of my prize winning chili for dinner instead of you having to cook again?"

Charlotte opened her mouth in surprise. Could she be this lucky?

"I do like your cooking, Miss," Bill told her, "but chili sounds just fine on a cold, snowy day."

"Yes it does!" Davis agreed, looking to her for an answer. "What do you say, Charlotte, do you mind?"

The sound of him saying her name sent another zing through her stomach and Charlotte had two realities hit her hard at the exact same moment. First, she was going to survive her first day of being a fake chef without Bella at her side, which was rather unbelievable. Second, and this was even more shocking, she liked Davis. Not just as a nice person, but as a goofily handsome, unshaven, funny, kind, sweetheart of a man who she found incredibly attractive.

"No, I don't mind at all," she answered, her heart fluttering a little in her chest.

She didn't mind. She also didn't know how she could continue lying to Davis when all he had shown her was kindness, and she still didn't know what she was going to do when, or if, the guests showed up.

CHAPTER 5

Decorating with Davis was the most fun Charlotte had experienced in a while. They decided which ornaments to set aside to trim the tree, then got busy finding tables and shelves where they could set up the other Christmas knick knacks.

Davis was sweet, always at her side doing the heavy lifting and helping with anything she couldn't reach, which was plenty. They got so used to standing close together to accomplish a task that bumping into one another was no longer a big deal. Not entirely, anyway.

She liked the way it felt to have him near. She liked the sound of his voice in her ear when he was standing behind her, the way he cracked jokes and laughed easily, and the way he smelled. She really liked the way he smelled, like fresh cut firewood, cotton dried in the sun, and just the slightest hint of honey.

Soon they were done and the inside of the Inn looked almost as magical as the snow covered outside. Night had fallen and the little white lights were brilliant against an unthinkable amount of snow. They were warm and cozy at the kitchen table eating chili and Charlotte was trying to decide if she could continue this way. Should she tell Davis that she was not who she claimed to be?

She had taken one fake smoke break before dinner to talk to Bella, who was still a day's drive away without taking the highway closures into account. Charlotte determined there was no way she could keep up the facade even if she wanted to. Bella was alarmed at the idea.

"Charlie, you can't tell anyone!"

"It took me over two hours to fix lunch, Bella. It's not fair to lead Davis on and let him think I'm going to impress these people, because I'm not," Charlotte argued.

"What if he tells the network?"

Charlotte hadn't thought about that. Admitting the truth to Davis was the right thing to do, and it was scary to think how he might react. But the thought of being exposed as a fraud to the world made her stomach sink.

Bella continued, "We have six months left on the show. Then we just don't sign a new contract and we go on with our lives. If they find out before that we could be fired, or sued!"

Charlotte hesitated, maybe Bella was right. She chewed her lip and thought about the possible consequences, her stomach roiling with stress.

"Charlie?" Bella waited for her reassurance.

"I just..." Charlotte looked back towards the Inn with its Christmas decorations, so welcoming in the night. She sighed.

"Promise me you're not going to tell him," Bella demanded.

"Okay," the word came out like a squeak. A spineless, fearful sound.

"What?"

CHARLOTTE'S CHRISTMAS CHARADE

"I said 'Okay'," Charlotte answered, louder this time.

Sitting at the table with Davis and Bill, Charlotte nibbled at her chili. It was hot and actually quite tasty, but she didn't have much of an appetite. She'd promised Bella, but there had to be some way she could warn Davis of her incompetence in the kitchen before she ruined his big plans for the holiday.

"You don't like it?" Davis asked, dropping his gaze to her bowl of chili then back up to her, a little crestfallen.

"Oh, no, I mean, yes. It's very good," she tried to smile and took a little bite.

"The snow's all but stopped," Bill chimed in. He looked out the window at the night. The yard light shone down from above revealing huge drifts of snow, but no snowflakes falling.

"Good, maybe they'll make it after all," Davis looked from the window down into his bowl. They were all quiet for a moment, pondering the arrival of the guests from their individual viewpoints. Then Davis wondered out loud, "What kind of name is Biddlebump do you think?"

Charlotte cracked a real smile.

Encouraged by her reaction, Davis continued, "What do you think their first names are? Buford and Belinda? Beaurigard and Beatrice?" He slipped in a southern accent on the second set of names.

Charlotte giggled.

"That is quite a name," Bill said, chuckling. "I guess we'll find out as soon as they open the roads."

"When do you think that might be?" Charlotte ventured the question that was weighing on her mind.

"Oh, might still be a few days. It depends," Bill mused.

Charlotte nodded and felt somewhat better.

Later, as she changed into her pajamas in her room and crawled under the covers, she still felt like a big jerk. All of the fun and excitement of decorating with Davis and getting to know him better was overshadowed by a giant cloud of anxiety and lies. She wanted to confess, just blurt out the truth and get it over with, not have this stupid lie to cover up all of the time. Maybe he could get a different cook from nearby to come to the Inn and take care of the guests.

Her mood perked up at the thought. Of course the Inn had to have a regular cook, didn't it? Surely he didn't let guests fend for themselves for their meals.

That's when Charlotte had a brilliant idea.

She would feign being sick. As sick as Bella had been when this whole mess had started at the cooking show audition. He wouldn't want her infecting the food and she would suggest that he bring in his regular cook. They would refund the money to him because she couldn't complete her part of the agreement, of course. That wasn't her concern right now. She needed to get out of having to cook while maintaining the facade that she actually could cook. At the same time she needed to make sure Davis got what he needed for the Inn to pass muster with the Fosters and the oddly named Biddlebumps.

The memory of Davis trying to guess their first names made her smile. This new plan was already making her feel better, lighter. Why hadn't she thought of this before? It was so easy it almost took care of itself. In the morning before she went downstairs she would work on her "sick" look and maybe even make fake vomiting sounds in her tiny bathroom for good measure.

Pleased with her new plan, she drifted off to sleep.

Shouting and the loud roaring of some kind of engine woke her from her slumber. She sat up and could vaguely make out men's voices yelling and, she wasn't completely sure, but she thought she heard a dog barking. When she looked out her window, she could just see the edge of what looked like a bright yellow tractor in the front drive.

The cold air went right through her pink flannel pajamas. She didn't have a robe, so grabbed the blue blanket off of her bed and wrapped it around her shoulders. By the time Charlotte got downstairs there was quite a commotion in the foyer and just outside the open front door. Pulling the blanket tighter around her shoulders, she peeked into the room.

Davis must have dressed in haste. He wore jeans, his boots, and his jacket, but his chest was bare underneath. He was lugging two large suitcases towards where she stood in the doorway. Following him was a small figure completely bundled in a white snowsuit with fur-trimmed hood that was pulled all the way over their face. From the size and style of dress, Charlotte assumed this was a woman, but she couldn't be sure. The edge of the yellow Snowcat was visible through the open door, its engine noise extremely loud, its piercing headlights illuminating the drifts of snow and shooting into the foyer.

Davis looked up and saw her standing there with her blanket. He stood up straighter and smiled. She saw glimpses of dark hair over his muscled chest that made her lose track of what she was going to say.

"Good morning," Davis said, his eyes twinkling. Unshaven, with his dark locks truly out of control from springing straight from bed, he was so sexy and inviting that she fumbled for an answer. "They're here!" He continued, sweeping his arm to indicate the snowsuit figure behind him.

The figure pulled back their hood to reveal a head of red-blonde hair so brilliant in color Charlotte knew it was certainly dyed. It was a woman.

"Hello!" The woman said, smiling brightly and squinting at Charlotte through foggy glasses. She carried what looked like a hot pink pillow in her arms, but the pillow was squirming and growling.

Before Charlotte could answer, another figure, slightly larger and wearing a snowsuit that matched the woman's except it was completely black, pushed their way into the foyer. They carried another squirming pillow, this one in neon blue.

"What a trip!" A man's voice came out of the black fur.

The Snowcat roared its engine again, pulling away from the Inn. Bill stepped into the foyer and closed the door. He was just as disheveled as Davis, except his jacket was completely buttoned and she assumed he was wearing a shirt underneath. The snowsuit couple placed their squirming pillows on the floor where they started wriggling and running around in circles.

"These are the Foss'," Davis announced while gesturing towards the newcomers. "And this is Charlo–Chef Charlotte!" He swept his arm back to indicate Charlotte, who was now shivering in her bare feet on the cold floor.

"Hello!" The black snowsuit pushed back his hood to reveal the partially bald, very square head of Dennis Foss. He, too, wore glasses that were fogging up from the change in temperature. He took them off and looked at her with sharp, intelligent eyes. "Denny Foss," he stuck out his hand and stepped towards Charlotte who took it and was not shocked at the very firm handshake. "My wife, Vicky," Denny indicated the woman, who waved at Charlotte happily.

Charlotte gave a short wave back and her best early morning smile. Then she looked around expectantly, "Did the Biddlebumps decide not to come?"

Denny and Vicky looked at her then at each other. Vicky bent down to grab the pink wiggling pillow at her feet as Denny looked back at Charlotte and gave her a full tooth smile, "They're right here." He swooped down and picked up the turquoise pillow.

"This is Mrs. Blanche Biddlebump," Vicky unzipped the pink doggie snowsuit to reveal an excited, panting Pug, tan with a black face and crazy bug eyes.

"And this is Mr. Bernie Biddlebump," Denny announced, revealing an all black Pug in the other suit. He had the same bug eyes, the same wriggling excitement. Denny smiled, his straight, white teeth beaming at her, "They're married."

CHAPTER 6

The lively group retired to the kitchen where Charlotte made coffee. Denny regaled them with the story of how he, his wife, and their married Pugs commandeered a giant yellow Snowcat to drive them through icy roads buried in snow so they could make it to the Inn. Davis assisted Charlotte in grabbing mugs, and cream and sugar, for the table. As he stood next to her, his jacket still draped over his shirtless torso, Charlotte admired his physique with small, sideways glances.

With everyone safely out of hearing distance, Davis leaned in to her ear and whispered, "The Biddlebumps are dogs!"

Charlotte fought back a laugh. Davis looked completely befuddled and amused.

"I see that," she said.

He made a 'who knew' face as he hooked his fingers into several mug handles to pick them up. He thought of something and leaned in towards her ear again. Charlotte could feel his breath on the skin of her neck, sending a small shiver through her body.

"At least we know their first names now," he whispered.

Denny and Vicky were delightful. Both dentists, they had the kind of super fit and put together look of people who have taken very good care of themselves for a very long time. Great hair, great skin, really great teeth. They were in their fifties, Charlotte guessed, described themselves as happily child free and had obviously turned any parental urges they did have towards their dogs.

The Biddlebumps were absolutely adorable. They snuffled around the kitchen, exploring underneath the table and in every corner of the room, and running back to check in with their owners every few minutes. Charlotte was smitten with their little faces, so ugly they were cute. She was also glad they were different colors, because she didn't think she could tell them apart otherwise.

"Alex was a doll to bring us," Vicky gushed, picking Blanche up off of the floor and snuggling into the rolls of skin around the Pug's almost nonexistent neck. She was talking about the Snowcat driver who, apparently, they'd become fast friends with on the ride.

Denny gave his wife a piercing look, not in displeasure, more like a look of intense admiration. Denny, Charlotte had noticed, looked at everything like he was boring a hole into it with his eyes.

"I think someone has a little crush on Alex," he teased.

Vicky laughed and it was a big sound, filling the room and making it impossible not to laugh along.

"Do you mean me or Blanche?" She asked.

"Both!" Denny exclaimed, "I do believe both my girls would take off with Alex in that machine of his and drive into a blizzard if he invited them." He patted the side of his leg and Bernie waddled happily to him. Denny pet the little black dog's round head, "Good boy, Bernie. At least you would stick with me."

The new arrivals in the Inn were so animated and amusing that the coffee probably wasn't even necessary for everyone to wake up, but it did add a sense of camaraderie. Charlotte was reminded of when she was little and her parents would sit in the kitchen and visit with neighbors or friends who had just stopped by to say 'hi'. The kitchen and the company were warm, pleasant, and homey.

She caught Davis looking at her a few times. When she saw him he would smile sweetly and drop his gaze to his coffee or back to Denny, who did most of the talking in their little group. These tiny stolen moments with Davis put her in a state of pure happiness. She had that buzz that happens on a really great first date.

Dawn broke and the sun spilled over the snow-covered landscape outside the kitchen window. As the sun's rays grew stronger they created a sparkling wonderland, like a snow fairy had scattered diamonds across the rounded drifts as far as the eye could see.

"Oh my God, it's beautiful!" Vicky exclaimed.

"Let's get a picture," Denny jumped up from the table and there was a bustle of excitement.

"I'm gonna throw some more clothes on first," Davis said. Charlotte had a flicker of disappointment because his nicely formed chest was going to be out of view, then realized that she needed to change as well.

"Me too," she announced.

"Then you'll join us outside for a picture?" Denny asked, more like strongly suggested.

"Sure," Davis answered, looking at her for approval.

"Yes, of course," she agreed.

Upstairs she hurried through a quick morning routine including braiding her long, dark hair into a thick French braid. She put on a pair of jeans and a green plaid print baby doll style shirt. In the foyer she pulled on her black snow boots and her jacket, then joined the group outside.

The sunshine was so bright, Charlotte had to squint to see anything.

"Here," Davis walked up to her and pulled a pair of sunglasses out of his coat pocket, handing them to her. He already had a pair on, which gave him a hunky ski instructor look.

"Thanks," she said, putting on the glasses.

"I always keep extras for guests. Nobody expects it to be so bright up here, but you can go snow-blind if you're out in this too long."

"Really?" She looked around through the glasses, much better.

"Are you two ready?" Vicky called to them. She waved them over to join her and Bill at a spot in front of the Inn.

Denny was setting up a tripod in the driveway and had a black case next to him that Charlotte suspected held a very expensive camera.

"Hold the Biddlebumps," Denny instructed. "I don't want them messing up the snow too much."

Vicky picked up Bernie who already had tiny snowballs sticking to his belly and leg fur. Davis reached out to help her and she handed the happy little Pug to him. Then she gathered Blanche up in her own arms. They stood in a group for the photo, with Denny watching through his camera eyepiece and shouting out instructions until they were in perfect position. The whole time Bernie Biddlebump kept trying to lick Davis' chin. When he grew bored with that, he made grunting noises as he attempted to reach Charlotte's face to give it a good lick. Charlotte could hear Davis chuckling at the dog's antics.

"Ready!" Denny cried, then ran towards them and placed himself next to his wife.

"Do we smile?" Bill asked from his position at the back of the group.

"Yes," Denny said between his teeth, holding his smile in place. "Smile and don't move."

They all held still and smiled at the camera, except for the Biddlebumps. The little dogs seemed to sense Denny wanted them to hold still and, like small children, this made them even more rambunctious. Bernie panted and flung his head back and forth between Davis and Charlotte, trying desperately to get into licking range. Davis held his smile in place, but Charlotte could feel his shoulders shaking as he laughed at the little dog.

Finally, Denny released them from their pose and checked the images on his camera. Declaring the picture 'excellent', he dismissed them to do as they pleased.

Davis put Bernie on the ground where he immediately plunged his face into the snow, sniffed heartily, and began sneezing. Davis laughed out loud.

"Watch out, buddy, you're gonna get a brain freeze," he said to the dog. Bernie looked up at him with snow covering his snout and wagged his butt, because he had no tail to speak of. Davis shook his head, chuckling.

"They are so cute!" Charlotte exclaimed, watching the Pugs play in the snow.

"They are," Davis agreed. "Do you have dogs?"

"No, I love dogs, though," she answered. "I haven't had the free time to take care of one on my own. We always had dogs growing up."

"Yeah, me too," he said. "I wanted to get a Lab. I think a Lab would be great out here," he waved his arms towards the barn and the pine trees beyond. "Although these guys seem to be enjoying it, too," he reached down to scratch Bernie's little head.

"But you don't have one?"

"Naw," he stood up and shook his head, then looked out into the distance. "My ex didn't want a dog. I do know someone who's Lab had a litter recently. I thought about bringing one of those home, but..." he looked at Denny and Vicky who were enrapt by something Bill was saying, "I didn't want to take on the responsibility right now, since I wasn't sure what was going to happen with this place."

She couldn't read his expression since he was wearing sunglasses, but he sounded sad. She looked at Denny and Vicky.

"They seem to be having a good time so far," she said, hoping to sound encouraging.

He flashed her a smile, "So far so good!"

"Exactly."

"I'm gonna take them on a little tour of the place, the barn and everything. Do you want some help with breakfast?" He asked.

Breakfast! Her stomach knotted up. She had forgotten to play sick! And now it was time for breakfast.

Charlotte's answer caught in her throat, making it sound squeaky, "No, I'll be fine. I'll get started on it now."

She turned on her heel and headed inside without another word. The whole time her mind was racing. How could she be so stupid? She couldn't suddenly come down with the flu after laughing and talking all morning over coffee then grinning like an idiot next to Davis in the freezing cold. She stripped her outerwear off in the foyer, the happy group of glowing Santas watching her with their collectively goofy expressions.

She glared at them and said, "Yeah, real funny."

She hurried down the hall towards the kitchen then changed her mind and went up to her room to get her cell phone. She would have to call Bella again, but with the tour going on outside it was going to be almost impossible to go to her normal spot in the drive to talk to Bella without raising suspicion. She flew into her room and grabbed her phone from the nightstand, swiping the screen with her finger to wake it up. No response.

"No!" She covered her mouth with her hand, trying not to panic.

Her phone was dead. Charlotte pressed the ON button again. Nothing. Just a black screen.

"No-no-no-no-no..." she followed the charger cord with her eyes and saw that she hadn't gotten it plugged firmly into the outlet behind her bed last night.

Charlotte turned in a circle, one hand still covering her mouth, her dead phone in her other hand. What was she going to do?

"Okay," she took her hand off her mouth and breathed deeply through her nose, "calm down." Saying the words almost helped, but her heart was pounding and her palms were sweaty. She breathed in again through her nose and blew slowly through her mouth. Eggs, she thought. What's breakfast? Just some eggs and toast, right? She could definitely make toast. What kind of eggs? Scrambled. Scrambled eggs would be easiest. She'd made scrambled eggs before, they hadn't turned out great, but maybe there were enough condiments and other toppings she could put out to distract everyone. And coffee. She wasn't worried about coffee.

In the kitchen, the group thankfully still outside, Charlotte opened the giant stainless steel refrigerator. It was packed. She looked at all of the raw ingredients, much of which Davis bought because she and Bella had requested it, and her eyes grew wide.

"Focus," she muttered, zeroing in on cartons of eggs stacked on a shelf and grabbing the top one. She gathered what she thought she might need on the counter: a frying pan, eggs, butter, salt and pepper. Nothing fancy. Just the basics.

Thirty minutes later Charlotte had a bowl of mostly edible scrambled eggs sitting on the table. She'd only had to throw one batch away. They had turned out slimy, so she tried again. She found some cheddar cheese that she shredded, almost cutting her fingernail off during the process. But she put the shredded cheese on top of the second batch of eggs and thought they would work. She made several pieces of toast, thanking God for toasters and their reliability the entire time. She found salsa, a red one and a green tomatillo variety, mango chutney, raspberry jam, apple butter and orange marmalade.

Using some of the china she'd found in boxes the day before, she set the table. The pattern on the plates were of poinsettias and they had darling little matching cups and saucers. With red cloth napkins she'd found in the linen drawer and the jars of condiments placed in the center, the table was bright and cheery, especially with the view of the glittering snow outside. She felt better. Half of the experience of eating was visual, right?

"Oh, it's beautiful!" Vicky exclaimed as she came into the kitchen, "I hope you didn't go to too much trouble, we're not always big breakfast people." She squeezed Charlotte's arm. The Biddlebumps scampered in and ran around her feet, closely followed by the three men, then they all sat down to eat.

Breakfast went well...at first.

It turned out Denny and Vicky never ate much breakfast after traveling. They happily sipped coffee and nibbled on a few pieces of toast, much to Charlotte's relief. Davis and Bill took some eggs. After taking his first bite, Charlotte swore Davis frowned slightly, but hoped it was just her imagination. Bill had a healthy appetite, having seconds on everything, and thirds on coffee. After the first few minutes, Charlotte was relaxed enough to take a bite of the eggs.

Salt. That's all she could taste. No eggs, no cheese, just salt.

She tried to control the grimace on her face by biting into a piece of toast slathered in butter and marmalade, followed by a quick swig of coffee to wash the salt out of her mouth. Her eyes automatically shot to Davis, who was watching her, his eyebrows slightly lifted. She flicked her eyes to his plate then back up to him. He'd tasted it too, she knew. He hadn't touched the eggs on his plate since his first bite.

Heat filled her cheeks and she knew she looked red and embarrassed. How could she have added that much salt? It was horrible and burning and still stuck to her tongue. She took another sip of coffee while avoiding Davis' eyes. Bill was scraping his plate clean. He must not have taste buds, that was the only explanation.

Charlotte stood up, suddenly wanting to leave the room and take the bowl of hideously over salted eggs far from everyone. She picked up her plate and the eggs as if she was clearing the table.

"Can I help you with that?" Davis asked, very much the gentleman.

"No," she said quickly. "Thank you, I'm fine," she tried to act nonchalant as she took the bowl of eggs to the trashcan and discreetly scraped them on top of the first batch that she'd tossed.

Rinsing the dishes at the sink Charlotte knew there was no way she was going to get away with this. She couldn't risk ruining another meal and it wasn't fair to Davis to not tell him the truth. She would tell him that she couldn't cook and he would have to find someone else to come in and impress Denny and Vicky. It was the only thing she could do.

Only one question remained, when would she make her confession?

CHAPTER 7

W hen she was up in her room trying to call Bella, Charlotte thought of a dozen different ways to tell Davis the truth. First, she wanted to warn Bella what she was about to do, and maybe part of her hoped her friend would talk her out of it. There was no answer. Her call went straight to voicemail. She didn't leave a message.

Downstairs, she found Davis alone, sitting in the living room flipping through what looked like ledgers.

"Are the Foss' here?" She asked.

"No," he closed the ledger in his lap. "They're in their room resting."

She nodded and sat down on the other side of the couch, "Is Bill around?"

A smile played on his lips as he shook his head 'no', "Feeding the horses."

She nodded again. Well, this wasn't awkward at all.

"Davis," saying his name made her feel strange and she paused, forgetting everything she'd rehearsed in her mind earlier.

"Yeah?" He watched her, waiting patiently.

"Davis...I..." again the words stuck in her throat. This was much harder to do than she'd anticipated.

Davis smiled knowingly and leaned forward, placing the ledgers on the coffee table, then turning on the cushion so he was facing her, one arm resting on the back of the couch.

"Davis–"

"I think I know what you want to say," he interrupted.

"You do?"

"I do," he ducked his head a little and looked up at her, his big, blue eyes especially dreamy. "I think...I think that maybe you and I are feeling a little," he pointed a finger back and forth between them, "chemistry?" His voice rose on the last syllable, making it more of a question than a statement. The cocky way he said it made it clear he thought there was no question at all.

Charlotte was stunned for a moment. This was unexpected.

Davis slid his hand over the couch, taking her hand in his gently. Her palms were sweaty from anxiety, not exactly romantic.

"I don't know if this is such a great time," he said. "With the Foss' here and this place," he let his eyes leave hers for a moment and glanced around the room. He sighed and squeezed her hand, "This place is in such trouble right now I don't think I can really focus on...any kind of romance."

Was he rejecting her? Was that even possible? Dumping her before there was an actual relationship?

"No," she pulled her sweaty hand out of his.

"I just think it would be better to keep everything profes-sional," he looked genuinely sad.

"I'm not–"

"I'm sorry," he interrupted.

"I can't cook!"

She blurted it out just like that. No full explanation of her and Bella's unfortunate situation. No lead in with anything that might help him understand. No filters.

His forehead wrinkled in confusion as he cocked his head, "What?"

"I can't cook. I'm not a chef," she spoke lower now, worried the others might walk in at any minute.

"You're not Chef Charlotte?" He sat back, suspicion on his face, no longer the nice guy trying to tactfully get out of dating her.

"I am Chef Charlotte," her face was red now. The humiliation of admitting everything to him had combined with being rejected and she was blushing furiously, "I have a show about cooking, but I can't cook. I don't actually do the cooking on the show."

He searched her eyes, processing the information. The entirety of her deceit clicked through his mind. Then he gave her an incredulous look.

"What?!" The word came out like a cough, like he couldn't breathe properly to get his voice out.

"I'm sorry. It wasn't supposed to be this way. My assistant, Bella, the one who missed her flight, she's the one who does everything. She's the one who knows everything. I'm just..." she searched for a word, "...the star."

"The star. The star?!" His voice rose with each word. He stood up, then sat back down and looked at her, then stood back up.

"It's a secret. It's been a secret from the beginning of the show. A big mistake when we auditioned and–"

"Wait," he stopped. "Nobody knows?"

She shook her head, "No."

Charlotte slumped into the couch, ashamed, wanting to sink into the cushions and disappear. Davis was stunned and confused, but she could see anger flickering across his face. He started pacing, running his hand through his floppy dark locks. She sat quietly, twisting her hands together in her lap.

"I guess that explains the eggs," he muttered under his breath. She almost laughed, but held it back. She didn't think he was trying to be funny.

"I thought maybe," she started speaking and he stopped pacing, turning towards her in a fast jerk like he had forgotten she was sitting there. "I thought maybe you have another cook that you could use instead, because Bella is having to drive here, but it's taking so long and with the roads closed..." her voice trailed off. He looked at her with a wild-eyed stare, his hair shooting off in all directions.

"What?" His voice was curt, angry.

"Do you," she cleared her throat, nervous at his outrage, "Do you have a regular cook?"

He gave her an exaggerated nod, "Yes! Of course I do. We're an Inn!" He raised his hands up like a maestro directing an orchestra. "But I gave our cook Christmas off and she went to Florida to visit family, because Chef Charlotte herself was going to be here!" He barked out a humorless laugh, gesturing towards her with both hands before letting them drop to his sides.

"Oh," she didn't know what else to say.

"Yes, 'oh'!" The comment was biting, sarcastic.

Davis put both of his hands over his face. Charlotte watched him silently, wishing she could do something, console him, offer a better plan, fall through the floor. He sucked a deep breath in through his fingers and held it, then let it out as he slid his hands down his face pulling his cheeks downward as he did. Without looking at her or saying anything else, he turned and walked out of the living room. Charlotte could hear him rustling in the foyer, then the front door slammed so hard it made her flinch.

She spent the next three hours in her room. Bella still

hadn't called her, which was probably for the best. Charlotte didn't want to talk to her right now. She'd betrayed their secret. She'd spent two days lying to Davis and possibly putting his business in peril. This was a huge mess and the blame sat squarely on her shoulders. She should have told Davis immediately that she couldn't go through with her end of the bargain. She shouldn't have agreed with Bella to be fake Chef Charlotte in the beginning.

Charlotte sighed. She was on her back on the bed, staring at the ceiling, wishing she were somewhere else. Her stomach growled. She looked at her phone, it was 11:30. Almost time for lunch. Great.

Guilt pressed down on her and she dropped her phone on the bed, sighing again. What else could she do? She had to carry on as if she was Chef Charlotte. People were expecting her. People were hungry. Convincing herself that there was probably some cold lunchmeat and cheese in the refrigerator that she could serve, Charlotte washed her face with cold water and made her way to the kitchen.

Once again she stood in front of the open door of the giant stainless steel refrigerator, anxiety rising in her chest as she looked at all of the food that she didn't know how to prepare. She pulled open the deli drawer and, glory be, saw a package of sliced roast beef and one of ham. She gathered those plus the block of cheddar cheese that she'd partially used this morning and turned to put them on the island behind her.

Davis was standing opposite her on the other side of the island, looking deflated.

"Oh!" She cried, startled at the sight of him, almost dropping her sandwich fixings.

"Sorry," his mouth scrunched into a half smile.

"I thought maybe I could make sandwiches...or something...for everyone..." Charlotte's voice got quieter. Her throat tightened and hot tears pressed on the back of her eyes. Her lower lip trembled a little as she spoke, "I'm sorry, I didn't mean for this to happen. Bella was supposed to be with me. It was going to be fun." A fat tear escaped and rolled down her cheek.

Davis let his chest sink and he put his elbows on the island, leaning forward, "Don't cry, please don't cry."

She sniffled, putting the food on the island and wiping the tear from her face with the cuff of her shirt.

Davis looked beat, like he'd been up all night. He let his head drop so all she could see were his thick, wavy locks. When he spoke, he spoke towards his clasped hands on the island counter.

"Just tell me one thing," he looked up at her. "And you have to promise it's the truth."

"Okay, I promise. I have no more secrets," she assured him.

"Did my ex put you up to this?"

"What?"

"My ex-wife. She's the one that hired you, or Bella I guess, right after last Christmas. She said it would bring in more customers," he watched her, tried to read her expression. Charlotte got the distinct feeling he wanted to believe in her.

"She did? I didn't know that," Charlotte answered. "Bella made all of the arrangements. But the answer to your question is 'no', your ex-wife has nothing to do with it." He took in her answer and stood up, giving her another scrunched smile. Charlotte was curious, "Why would you think she would sabotage you like that?"

He lifted one shoulder and let it drop, "Since I inherited this house she has no claim on it in our divorce. But, if the business fails and I can't pay on the loans it will force me to sell and through a whole mess of legal mumbo jumbo she will be entitled to a lot of the money."

"Oh," Charlotte said. How awful.

"But," he stood up straight and clapped his hands together. "I'm not giving up and, apparently, you're not giving up either," he gestured towards the sandwich fixings.

"No, I won't give up," she answered, relieved that he seemed to be over his initial anger and was moving on to being resourceful. "I'm not sure how much help I can be, though," she added guiltily.

"I think sandwiches for lunch sound great," he declared. "We need to feed everyone, then we're going snowshoeing to cut down a Christmas tree. So, all we need to worry about is a plan for dinner."

"Right," Charlotte answered, knitting her eyebrows in concentration. "What's good and hearty and warms you up after snowshoeing?"

Davis gave her a blank look. He was thinking hard. As was she.

"Hearty, tasty and warms you up..." Davis repeated. Then his eyes lit up. They both gasped at the same moment as they shared the same thought and said it out loud together.

"Chili!"

CHAPTER 8

M aking Davis' famous chili consisted mostly of emptying cans of ingredients into a crockpot. He did get out a white onion and a few pounds of ground chuck, saying it needed to be cooked and spiced before going into the crockpot. He saw the trepidation on Charlotte's face.

"You really don't know how to do any of this?" The question wasn't said in anger, but in disbelief.

"It's not necessarily that I don't know how to do it, it's just when I try it turns out badly," she sucked breath in through her teeth, "really badly."

Davis chopped the onion and sautéed it before adding the hamburger and spoonfuls of a crimson colored spice mixture out of a dark green tin can. While he did that, Charlotte opened cans of diced tomatoes, kidney beans and pinto beans, dumping them into the crockpot.

"How do you get away with that on your show?" Davis wondered out loud.

"Close ups," Charlotte quipped.

He laughed, then looked at her with disbelief, "Really?"

"Yes, really," she said, then thought about it some more. "That's not the only thing, though. We use really cool music and the lighting is just beautiful, like at an exclusive restaurant, you know?" Davis stirred the hamburger and listened with interest. She continued, "Bella is always there with me and everything is pre-chopped in little bowls. We have the most beautiful china and stoneware to use. Bella and I talk and joke a lot. Then I read from a script and they lay the audio over the final edit as a voiceover. But Bella mostly gives notes on the script for the producers. Of course, they think it's all coming from me," she kept talking as she took the cans to the sink, rinsed them quickly and put them in the recycling bin. "I guess they make the final show feel kind of like a fine dining party. Bella and I are always drinking wine, it's part of the vibe."

Davis turned off the stove and brought the browned beef and onions to the crockpot. He was quiet as he spooned the mixture in with the tomatoes and beans. Charlotte watched him, wondering what he was thinking.

"Haven't you seen the show?" She asked.

"No," he finished what he was doing and carried the pan to the sink. "My ex did. She loved it."

"Oh," somehow that made Charlotte feel strange, like she was a friend of his ex-wife.

"No offense," he offered, "I don't watch a lot of TV." He turned to her with a keen look of determination, "What if we copy some of that?"

"Copy some of what?"

"Your show!" It was clear he had what he thought was a good idea bubbling to the surface of his mind.

"I don't understand."

"Why don't we make each meal into a party? You already have the decorating down. We'll play music!" Davis did a little dance. "And...and..." he searched for something to add

64

to his plan. He snapped his fingers and pointed at her, "We'll get them drunk!" Charlotte laughed at that. He waved his hand in the air as if erasing that idea, "Maybe not drunk, but we'll have wine and make sure they're having fun. We'll give them a party so they don't notice the food."

Charlotte was still smiling, watching him so animated was fun. His excitement was contagious and ideas on how they could make each meal an experience to remember flew through her mind.

Davis paused and watched her, waiting for an answer. His eyes had that adorable twinkle again and she was so happy that not only was he apparently forgiving her falsehoods, but he was inviting her to take on this challenge with him. They would handle this problem as a team.

"What do you think?" He asked.

"I think it's a great idea!"

His face lit up and he moved towards her quickly, taking her up into a big hug. Davis was quite a bit taller than her, which meant that when they embraced, Charlotte was completely enveloped in his arms, her cheek against his chest. She was overwhelmed by his gentle strength. The feel of his chest, which she'd already had the chance to admire visually, combined with his sweet woodsy smell and she felt like she was tipping over some invisible edge into a lovely dream.

After a few moments in each other's arms, they separated rather quickly and more than a little awkwardly. The words he'd spoken earlier about having chemistry came tumbling back into her thoughts, but nothing was said. Davis gave her the shyest of smiles before stepping away.

"Do you want to go snowshoeing to get a tree?" He asked.

"Of course!" Was her giddy response.

THE THING ABOUT SNOWSHOEING, Charlotte quickly realized, was that it was really, really hard. Tromping through several feet of new snow, even if you were staying on top because of the huge attachments to your feet, still took a lot of strength and energy to move forward. Supposedly, the snowshoes distributed her weight evenly over a wider surface area, which kept her from sinking into the soft snow, like a snow leopard. She certainly didn't feel like a snow leopard.

"This is invigorating!" Denny shouted into the snow covered pine trees that surrounded them as he high kneed it far in front of the group. "Stop for a second," he yelled back at them, "I want to get a picture." He unstrapped his fancy camera bag from a small sled he was pulling that also held a chain saw and piles of rope.

Charlotte stopped happily, using the few extra minutes of rest to catch her breath. Davis and Vicky were just a few feet ahead of her. She wasn't sure if either of them were as exhausted as she was. Bill had stayed back with the Biddle-bumps, stating his trick knee and old heart probably couldn't take snowshoeing. She was so hot and sweaty that she wished she could take off her jacket, but knew the ice cold air could possibly make her sick, even if it felt glorious at first. Or was that an old wive's tale?

"Are you ladies doing okay?" Davis asked.

"I'm good," Vicky announced.

Charlotte was slightly jealous at the brightness in her voice.

"Fine," Charlotte answered, trying to act like she wasn't thinking this had been a terrible idea.

"Got it!" Denny yelled happily and waved them on.

The trudging commenced.

When Charlotte wasn't sure she could keep going forward and still have enough energy to return to the Inn, Davis declared they were in the best spot. The trees in this area were smaller than the giant pines they'd walked through. Davis approached each of them and hit their trunks with the handle side of a shovel, knocking the built up snow off of their limbs.

"Oh, these are gorgeous," Vicky declared, taking in the size and shape of each tree.

"I'm going to leave the picking of the tree up to you three," Davis announced. He went to the sled and started unstrapping the chainsaw, "I'll just do the cutting."

After about twenty minutes of comparison shopping, Denny, Vicky and Charlotte all agreed on a tall, slender Scotch pine tree whose branches seemed very full and well distributed.

The cutting of the tree took no time at all, but the tying it up with rope and strapping it to the sled seemed to take forever. Charlotte started to feel chilled, probably from all of the sweat drying on her skin. She was glad she hadn't given in to the urge to take her jacket off earlier.

They returned to the Inn almost three hours after they had left with a twelve-foot tall Christmas tree in tow and only minor sticky sap issues on their hands. Bill helped Davis and Denny take the tree into the barn to cut down properly tomorrow. Charlotte went with Vicky and the Biddlebumps to rest in the living room.

"Phew," Vicky exclaimed, flopping onto the couch and putting her shoeless feet up on the coffee table. "That was quite a workout, wasn't it?"

"Yes," Charlotte answered, happy to know Vicky wasn't in so much better shape than she was that she was immune to the effects of snowshoeing.

Blanche and Bernie snuggled at their feet and Charlotte was thankful Bill had started a fire for them while they were out. The smell of Davis' chili wafted through the room and she smiled to herself. Chili had been a good idea.

"So, I've been wanting to talk to you about your show," Vicky confided. Charlotte tensed. "I love it!" Vicky said, "It's so much fun to watch. Makes a person want to throw a party."

"Thank you, that's good to hear," Charlotte answered, glad she was a fan, but cautious about getting into details.

"Have you always wanted to be a chef?"

"Oh, not necessarily a chef," she hated this part. She would rather not lie, even though her entire existence depended on leading people to believe she was a chef. She used her technically correct, but meant to mislead answer, "But I do like throwing a good party."

"Isn't this place beautiful?" Vicky looked around the room in admiration. Charlotte agreed. "And the decorations are adorable. Those plastic Santas in the foyer are so kitschy, I love them! I've got a thing for that kind of trashy vintage look." Vicky admitted.

Saved by the men returning from the barn, Charlotte got up to start preparing to serve the chili. Her leg muscles were already sore, but she was glad she'd endured the grueling workout. She enjoyed the feeling of having accomplished such a big task and she definitely looked forward to trimming the tree.

She met up with Davis in the kitchen and they made their plan. They would serve the chili in the living room by the roaring fire. The Foss' were upstairs changing and while they were gone Davis dimmed the lights in the living room and lit several candles around the space. Charlotte got out heavy, off white stoneware bowls to serve the chili and chose some wine from the pantry, placing it on the island with wine glasses. Davis turned on some Christmas jazz music for ambience.

He popped his head into the kitchen, "Do you like the music?"

She grinned at him, "It's perfect." She was fixing a large

tray with all of the bowls ready to fill with chili along with napkins, silverware, a plate of saltine crackers, a bowl of grated cheddar cheese and a bowl of sour cream.

"We have this wine and also beer, if that's what they want," she told him.

"Great, let the chili party begin!"

Davis had only been half joking about keeping Denny and Vicky drunk to improve their experience. Although, in his defense, he didn't have to do much coercing to get them to partake of the available spirits. Vicky stuck with wine while Denny enjoyed a few different locally brewed ales that Davis had on hand. The chili was delicious, perfectly spiced, hot, thick and warmed them to the bones. The music was mellow and relaxing, and they had a wonderful time eating with each other in front of the fireplace.

When everyone was completely done eating, Davis excused himself to the kitchen and invited Charlotte to come with him. The kitchen was dark, illuminated only from the light in the hallway. She followed him in and they stood whispering by the freezer.

"I have something that might be good for dessert," Davis said.

Dessert? She'd forgotten all about dessert.

He opened the freezer and pulled out a two-gallon zipper top plastic bag full of oversized chocolate cookies.

"Our normal cook makes these for the kids when they come," he pulled one of the cookies out and Charlotte could see that it wasn't just a cookie.

"Ice cream sandwiches?" She asked.

"Yep, she makes the chocolate chip cookies then fills them with ice cream and freezes them," he gave her a questioning look. "Do you think that's good enough?"

"It's so kitschy," Charlotte said, giggling at her own joke. Davis didn't understand and looked a little worried. "I think they will love them," Charlotte assured him. "I'll make some decaf," she added.

"Excuse me, guys," Denny's voice came to them from the doorway, startling Charlotte where she stood. "Don't want to interrupt," Denny added, giving them a knowing grin.

"You're not interrupting," Davis leaned away from her a little bit, putting a proper amount of distance between them. "We're just getting out dessert."

"Great," Denny stepped into the kitchen. "I have something I need to confess to someone and I can't tell my wife," he said.

Charlotte was surprised, wondering if maybe they'd gotten Denny a little too drunk during dinner. She looked at Davis who gave her a sideways glance before answering.

"What's up?" Davis asked.

Denny came closer to them, checking behind him into the hallway to ensure Vicky wasn't nearby. Charlotte didn't know if she wanted to hear whatever he had to confess, but Davis was there with her and she trusted he wouldn't let things get too crass.

"I forgot Vicky's Christmas present," Denny whispered.

"Oh," Charlotte said, her discomfort easing.

Denny shook his head with dismay, "She warned me I was obsessing over my new camera equipment. I spent so much time packing and repacking it for our trip. Then I up and left her present laying on the bed."

"Man, that's tough," Davis said.

Denny was shaking his head, disgusted at himself, "I don't know what to do. Thirty years together I've never not had a gift for her on Christmas morning." His chiseled features and piercing eyes were fraught with true disappointment as he glared intensely at the tile on the island. It broke Charlotte's heart a little to see him so upset.

"Maybe I can help," Charlotte blurted out. Both of the

men looked at her with surprise. "I mean, maybe I can help you make something she might like. Not food," she clarified. "Something handmade that she can take home."

"Would you?" Denny was thrilled at the idea.

She smiled at him and at Davis, who was looking at her with a mixture of wonder and concern.

"I'll certainly try."

CHAPTER 9

Bella wasn't going to make it any time soon. Charlotte had to face that fact. She had harbored some hope that her friend's road trip would land her at the Inn sometime today, her third day there, and all would be saved, but they were having no such luck. Even though Bella had been on the road for two whole days, the bad weather was making it slow going. She hadn't even entered Colorado yet.

"Don't put yourself at risk," Charlotte told her friend. "Davis and I are working together on getting decent food on the table. It's not what you could do, but so far it hasn't been awful."

"I still cannot believe you told him," Bella said, put out with Charlotte since she'd admitted that fact earlier in their call.

"It was the right thing to do, Bella. He had a lot riding on making a good impression."

Bella sighed. It was a dramatic sigh and Charlotte imagined Bella smacking her forehead with her hand.

"I hope he doesn't blab it to the world," Bella complained.

"He won't," Charlotte was almost positive he wouldn't give away their secret. "You just be careful driving. Do you think you'll come here or try to go back home for the holiday?"

"I'm coming there! You can't have toast and–and–canned chili for Christmas dinner."

That was true and Charlotte was thankful that Bella was intending on being here at some point. If they could just keep up a good show until she arrived to do the real cooking, everything would be fine.

Christmas dinner seemed far off as Charlotte and Davis made breakfast together.

"I'll start coffee, that's great for morning ambience," she offered.

"How is it you're so good at making coffee?" Davis asked.

"I don't know, it's a natural talent I have," she answered with a flirty sparkle.

"I see," Davis responded. "I have a few of those, but they don't have anything to do with the kitchen," he winked at her and little butterflies flitted around her stomach. "Are you good with bacon?"

She cocked her eyebrow at him. Was he still flirting? He held up a package of bacon, making her laugh out loud.

"If you show me what to do, I can manage," she told him. She thought she caught a little blush cross his cheeks at her innuendo.

Davis set her up to manage the bacon so he could get started on some French toast. They had agreed that dipping bread into eggs then frying it in butter seemed simpler than trying to tackle pancakes.

"Maybe we'll be old pros by tomorrow morning and we'll whip up some pancakes," Davis suggested with a hopefulness she was beginning to find endearing.

"Maybe," she said, still feeling saucy. "Or maybe we could try a quiche!"

He wrinkled his nose, "Not sure about quiche. Oh! I almost forgot!" Davis dug through the refrigerator for a minute and pulled out orange juice and a bottle of chilled champagne.

"Mimosas?" She cried with pleasure.

Breakfast was ready and looked glorious. Classical guitar music was the background music for the morning. Charlotte had chosen some adorable snowman dishes with blue and green edging to set the table. She'd also found an elegant crystal bowl that she put in the center of the table and filled with the vintage glass ornaments she'd found in the boxes. They were pale blue, lime green, pink, red and gold. Their glittering surfaces added an extra splash of festive to the table. As they waited for everyone to arrive for breakfast, she stood with Davis admiring the table and the gorgeous snow covered morning outside the windows.

"The only thing we're missing is a snowman outside to match these little guys," Charlotte said, touching one of the snowman plates.

Davis leaned over so he was closer to her ear, "Maybe we can do that." He touched her elbow when he said it and a shiver traveled up her arm and across her shoulders.

The Biddlebumps arrived first. Their tiny nails came clattering down the hallway and skidding around the corner as they raced each other into the kitchen. They were fresh from their morning outing. Still damp from jumping in the snow that was well above their heads along the edges of the path Bill had cleared just for them. The fresh cold air invigorated the little dogs, along with the knowledge that food was being served and, therefore, they were about to get a snack.

"Hi Blanche! Little Miss Beautiful," Charlotte reached down and rubbed her brown Pug head, noticing that Vicky had attached a tiny red bow using some kind of cosmetic glue. Bernie did not enjoy being ignored. He pushed his fat Pug face in between Blanche's head and Charlotte's hand, "Okay, Bernie, good morning to you, too." Charlotte laughed.

"It smells good in here," Bill commented. He came in the kitchen, smiling and good-natured as always. He was followed almost immediately by Vicky, then Denny.

"Coffee smells good," Denny said, giving them all a gleaming good morning smile.

"Mm, mimosas!" Vicky declared, heading straight for the champagne flutes filled with the fizzy brunch drink.

Charlotte looked at Davis and he gave her a slight nod, everything was ready.

"Dig in," she invited everyone to the table where they did, dig in. There were oohs and awes over the table settings. The bacon was a hit, as was the French toast, and even if some of the pieces hadn't been completely cooked through and had a tiny squish to them, nobody seemed to notice. Davis and Charlotte kept the conversation entertaining and the mimosas flowing. Blanche and Bernie even got to split their own piece of French toast with no syrup or butter. Denny and Vicky enjoyed giving their little dogs treats, and the Biddle-bumps didn't care if there were any uncooked bits.

When breakfast was over, Charlotte found a discreet moment to pull Denny aside.

"Denny, I have an idea of something we could possibly make for Vicky," Charlotte kept her voice low.

Denny's eyes flew open, he grabbed her hand warmly, "Do you? That would be fantastic! I don't want to be that husband, you know?"

They made a deal to meet in the foyer and go to the barn as soon as Vicky laid down for a nap, which would probably be very soon since she'd had four mimosas.

Davis had graciously taken all of the supplies Charlotte asked for to the workbench in the barn and turned on the small space heater so it would be warm enough. He'd even given her permission to use whatever vintage Christmas light bulbs she wanted for the project. When she and Denny set to work in the barn later that morning, he was over the moon excited.

"You don't know what this means to me," Denny told her, his intense gaze glittering with what she thought might be tears of gratitude.

"I hope she likes it," Charlotte warned him. "We have to use what we have on hand, which is a little limiting."

"Whatever we can do is better than what I have, which is nothing!"

Charlotte proceeded to show him her plan. She knew that Vicky liked the vintage look that she'd used in decorating the Inn, and she proposed that they make her a Christmas wreath decoration using the old Christmas bulbs that Davis no longer needed for the lights.

"Sounds perfect!" Denny gave her a thumbs up as he peered into the box of old bulbs, "I remember using these when I was a kid. I think she'll love it!"

Charlotte had Denny help her bend four wire coat hangers into circles, then wrap them around each other to form the wire frame of the wreath. They pinched the wire together with pliers, then carefully wrapped silver and gold tinsel garland around that base to create a background for the bulbs. Thankfully, Davis had found a glue gun in some of the general supplies his ex-wife left behind when they divorced. That had been the one piece Charlotte was worried about when she came up with this idea.

"Wait," Denny told her as she glued the first bulb into place, "I want to get a picture." Charlotte started to protest, but he stopped her, "Part of this present will be the fact that

Chef Charlotte herself made it for her, trust me, she'll love it even more knowing you had a hand in it."

She could see his point so allowed it. He gleefully took a picture of Charlotte smiling next to the not yet made wreath, then dove in with such dedication that the wreath was complete in less than an hour. After finishing this project with Denny, she could imagine him working diligently and precisely on someone's teeth. He was probably a really good dentist.

"Now we just take it in and wrap it up. I'll ask Davis if he has some extra wrapping paper somewhere," Charlotte said, pleased that Denny was so happy with the results.

Once inside, they hid the wreath in Davis' office where Vicky wouldn't be passing by and Denny went upstairs to take a little rest. But not until he gave her a warm hug and kissed her on the cheek, thanking her profusely for helping him.

When Denny disappeared up the stairs, Charlotte turned to find Davis leaning against the entry to the living room. His gaze held steady on her, a warm smile in his eyes.

"That was really sweet of you," he said.

She blushed a little, "It wasn't terribly hard, and he is so nice. They both are. I wanted to help."

"You seem to enjoy helping."

"I guess I do," she was warm and tingly, that great feeling after doing something that makes someone else happy.

"I need your help," he continued, giving her a mischievous look.

"You do?"

He nodded, "We need to figure out what's for lunch, and dinner, and breakfast, and lunch and dinner again!" He kept his voice at a whisper, but made it look like he was shouting at the rooftops.

"Don't panic," she laughed.

"I've got cookbooks coming out my ears!" He whisper

yelled again, pretending to pull on his hair in crazed frustration.

"Show me," she grabbed him by the arm and they went to the kitchen where they settled in to look through cookbooks at the kitchen table and come up with their ultimate Christmas cooking plan–for novices.

CHAPTER 10

By dinner the next night, Charlotte and Davis were in a real rhythm cooking together. Not only did they do a thorough review of all of the supplies Bella had requested for the holiday, but they also worked out simple, yet tasty menus for each meal using those delicious ingredients. Plus, and this was Charlotte's favorite part, they got really good at working side by side in the kitchen.

They always played music. Davis had a wide variety of music, including many different types of Christmas music. Since it was December 23rd and they were planning to trim the tree that evening, he declared they were only playing Christmas music from then on. And they always had fun drinks to mix and beautiful dishes and decorations to arrange. They had decided on chicken enchilada casserole for the tree trimming dinner, along with a green salad and a spice cake for dessert. The festive drink of the evening was eggnog, with a little dark rum and cognac added for kick.

Charlotte stood at the punch bowl, measuring out the eggnog and liquor then adding chunks of ice from the freezer. Davis was layering tortillas, cooked chicken, grated cheese and green chili sauce in a large casserole dish. The sleeves of his shirt were unbuttoned and pushed up his arms so he could work. His dark hair was just long enough to fall into his eyes, giving him a casual, unassuming look. Charlotte had already dimmed the lights and lit the candles in the kitchen and living room. The freshly cut pine tree was set up beside the living room fireplace, strung with lights and ready to be decorated. Its fresh pine scent hung heavy in the air.

It's Beginning to Look a lot like Christmas by Johnny Mathis had just ended when a deep thrumming beat began and the familiar song *The Little Drummer Boy* started to play. Charlotte was trying to remember if this was the original Bing Crosby version when, to her surprise, Davis started singing along.

"A new born king to see, pa rum pum pum pum," his voice was a deep bass. He glanced up and saw her listening to him, which only made him sing louder, "Our finest gifts we bring, pa rum pum pum pum!" He pulled open the oven door dramatically and pushed the casserole inside, "To lay before the king, pa rum pum pum pum, rum pum pum pum, rum pum pum pum." He half danced, half marched towards her, grabbing a wooden spoon and using it as a microphone. When he reached her, the tone of the song softened slightly so he leaned in as if he was crooning a ballad, "So to honor him, pa rum pum pum pum..."

A warm, syrupy feeling slipped through her as he sang. He was showing off, she knew that, and it made her glow. He had a great voice, so deep and with good tone. She wouldn't be surprised to find out he'd had some training. He held the spoon out to her and she sang a 'rum pum pum pum' into it. Encouraged by her participation, Davis took her hand and twirled her then they both sang the chorus of 'rum pum pum pums' into the spoon.

A clickety clacking sound interrupted them as the Biddlebumps skittered into the kitchen. They wiggled their round little bodies so hard Bernie almost fell over sideways.

"Whoa, Bernie, careful buddy," Davis told the little dog. At the sound of his name, Bernie jumped up so his front paws were on Davis' jeans. Davis leaned down to pet him, "I can't pick you up right now, buddy, I'm cooking."

Bernie and Blanche kept them company by scampering around their feet for the remainder of dinner preparations. Soon Denny, Vicky and Bill joined them and it was time for the festivities. They fixed their plates, loaded up on spiked eggnog and headed into the living room to trim the tree.

And a glorious tree it was.

Covered top to bottom with white lights and stretching almost to the ceiling the tree was more than twice Charlotte's height. When she stood next to it she felt like a little girl gawking up at the twinkling Christmas tree, letting her imagination run away with the magic of the holiday. As an adult she'd tried to recreate that feeling each year by throwing parties for her family and friends and diving into all of the holiday traditions with gusto. Tonight, snowed in by huge drifts, cozy and warm by the fire, with Davis nearby always attentive to her and trying to charm her, she thought that this was the first time in a long time she'd actually felt like Christmas held some real magic in it.

He stood next to her, their sides bumping into one another as they took ornaments out of a box on the floor and hung them on the tree. She held a particularly lovely ornament shaped like a Christmas star, all white with crystal glitter that reflected the lights. Charlotte had been eyeing a position on the tree that was still fairly open, but quite a bit out of her reach.

"Need some help?" Davis asked.

"Yes, please."

"Where do you want it?" He carefully took the fragile ornament from her hand, their fingers brushing as he did.

"Right there," she pointed.

Davis leaned in, placed his hand on the small of her back, and followed the direction she was pointing until he saw the spot. Charlotte's heartbeat sped up. His touch, so gentle, so familiar, was making her a little lightheaded. Or maybe it was the eggnog.

"There?" He asked, finding the spot exactly and hanging the ornament.

"Perfect," she answered.

"I think we're about done," Denny exclaimed, stepping back to get a look at the tree. "This is a damned fine Christmas tree. Come see," he waved Vicky to him and wrapped his arm around her waist as they stood admiring their decorating work.

Bill moved behind the couch and smiled at the tree, then at Davis, "This reminds me of the trees your Mom and Dad had."

Charlotte and Davis stepped back to look as well, and even though the tree was stunning, Charlotte missed the warmth of Davis' touch on her back. She wanted him to wrap his arm around her waist like Denny was with Vicky. She wanted them to be a couple.

"If you all would freshen up your drinks, I have something to show you," Davis told them. He looked at Charlotte and gave her a quick wink as he retreated to his office.

She filled her cup with more eggnog, because it was delicious and she loved the way it made her feel relaxed and smooth. They all sat down in the living room with the Biddle-bumps snuggled sweetly on Denny and Vicky's laps. Davis came back carrying a guitar.

"I thought maybe we should do some singing," he announced, sitting on the far end of the hearth.

"There you go," Bill said happily, raising his eggnog to Davis in a toast, "just like old times."

"You play?" Denny asked, moving to the edge of the couch, forcing Bernie to reposition.

"Yes, I haven't in a while, but I think I can work these rusty fingers for some Christmas carols," Davis answered, strumming the guitar once.

"It's too bad you didn't bring your guitar, honey," Vicky said, placing her hand on Denny's back.

"You play, too?" Davis asked, his face brightening.

"I do. Well, I try," Denny said humbly. Of course, they all knew Denny well enough by now to know that he didn't do anything halfway. Charlotte imagined he played quite well.

"Hang on," Davis stood, leaned his guitar against the wall and left the room, returning a few minutes later with another guitar. He handed it to Denny, who looked like he'd just been chosen to be on the team. Davis grinned and said, "Let's rock this place!"

And rock they did.

They started with *Frosty the Snowman* then went on to *Let it Snow*, *Blue Christmas*, *Santa Claus is Coming to Town*, and more. Denny's tenor voice blended perfectly with Davis and Bill's bass tones. Charlotte and Vicky joined in as the sopranos and, eventually, the Biddlebumps whined and howled along with the music. All in all, it was the happiest, most lively Christmas entertainment Charlotte could have imagined.

It grew later and later and Bill finally excused himself to get some sleep. Denny and Vicky followed soon after, taking the Pugs outside for a quick walk before bundling upstairs to bed. This left Charlotte on the couch feeling the sweet tingle of the great evening mingling with her multiple refills of spiked eggnog. Davis strummed the guitar from his seat on the hearth.

"Do you have a request?" He asked, looking up at her through his tumbling bangs.

"Oh, my, let me think," she said, furrowing her brow as she considered all of the possibilities.

Davis stood up and moved himself and his guitar to the open spot next to her on the couch.

"A personal concert?" She teased.

"Why, yes, ma'am. A song just for you," he answered. "Do you have one you want to hear?"

"How about White Christmas?"

"Done."

His fingers moved deftly across the strings, plucking and strumming, creating a beautiful intro to the song. Charlotte watched, enrapt with the lines of his jaw, the way he moved his chin ever so slightly in rhythm with what he was playing. Her stomach fluttered in anticipation of the deep, soft tones of his singing voice. He started the familiar song, "I'm dreaming of a White Christmas, just like the ones I used to know..."

He sang softer this time. No need to match Denny's enthusiasm in voice or playing now. He took his time, did everything right, let every word find its way out of his soul and resonate in her ear. He sang for her and her alone, and she never wanted it to end. She wanted to melt into him and let him wrap his voice around her until she fell asleep and then never, ever wake up from this dream.

When he finished, the last tones of the music dissipated in the air around them. Somehow they'd moved closer together, leaning towards one another while he sang. He dropped his head a little, suddenly bashful and uncertain. It was the most endearing move he could have made.

Charlotte reached out to him, placing her hand on his forearm. Without looking up, Davis readjusted his arm so he could catch her hand and hold it. He caressed her fingers with his thumb.

"That was...it was..." she couldn't think of a word to describe how the song made her feel.

He didn't wait. He pulled lightly on her hand, bringing her even closer as he used his other hand to slide the guitar out from between them. His eyes glittered with desire as he dipped his mouth towards hers. She tipped her face towards his, her eyes closing, impatient to feel their lips touch.

A familiar clickety clacking sound broke into their moment. Their eyes flew open and they moved away from each other, expecting to see Denny or Vicky walking into the living room. It wasn't Denny or Vicky. It wasn't polite little Blanche either. It was Bernie. Bernie Biddlebump had apparently escaped from the room upstairs and was full of joy over finding them in the living room.

"Bernie," Davis gave a semi-defeated laugh. "You have horrible timing, buddy."

Bernie responded by trying to jump on the couch between them while sniffling and whimpering his excitement.

The sound of Denny calling for Bernie and making his way downstairs to collect the little dog broke whatever spell they'd been under. Charlotte excused herself to go to bed. She didn't want Denny to find them together so late and so alone. Not that she was embarrassed exactly, it just seemed unprofessional. And after all of the work she and Davis had been doing to impress Denny and Vicky, perhaps it was better if they skipped a secret late night kiss...for now.

Still, as she drifted off to sleep in her bed, the way Davis looked at her and the sound of his voice played in a loop through her mind and she was sure that sweet dreams were on their way.

CHAPTER 11

The next day was Christmas Eve.

Charlotte and Davis started the morning early baking sugar cookies and gingerbread men to decorate. Charlotte was getting a little more confident with following recipes, but both of them knew Davis had more of a natural knack in the kitchen. Therefore, he was in charge of monitoring the cookie baking while Charlotte prepped the long kitchen table with all of the fun cookie decorating supplies Bella had the forethought to request.

They had all the colors in the rainbow to mix with buttercream frosting. They had red, green and chocolate sprinkles, tiny edible balls in silver, gold, white, and red, and a variety of different colored cookie decorating gel that squirted out of little tubes. They had gumdrops, red hots, licorice bits, round peppermint candies and chocolate kisses. Charlotte arranged these items in the center of the table and placed large platters within reach of every chair so they could set their freshly decorated cookies in a safe spot when they were done.

After breakfast, they all started on what quickly became a cookie decorating party. Bill declared that he wouldn't be good at decorating cookies, but he offered his services as the official cookie taster and consumer of broken pieces. It turned out that both the Biddlebumps had a thing for gingerbread and they were allowed a couple of small pieces.

Apprehensive about anyone noticing that she had less than professional frosting skills, Charlotte concentrated on doing very detailed work on her first cookie. It was a gingerbread man so she stuck with the classic white frosting trim, then added gumdrop buttons and used red hot candies for his eyes and mouth. She added some more white frosting flourishes, giving him pants and a little jacket and when she was done she thought it didn't look half bad.

"Look," Vicky held up her first sugar cookie that was in the shape of Santa Claus, but she'd decorated completely in blue frosting. "It's a Blue Man Group Santa," she said, giggling.

"I think mine looks like a troll," Denny said, showing them his gingerbread man that he'd decorated with green frosting and gel. "I was going for 'elf'," he confided.

"How about the Incredible Hulk?" Davis suggested.

Denny pointed at him, "You got it." He grabbed another undecorated gingerbread man from the waiting stack and went to town with the green frosting creating a Hulk cookie.

Davis turned his reindeer into a zebra, and then decided to make three more of them so there could be a herd of zebras. Charlotte worked on creating a couple of fairies and used the metallic colored edible balls and sugar glitter to give them extra sparkle. Denny made an entire superhero series of cookies, while Vicky focused on trying to create other famous characters like Forest Gump and the Doctor from Doctor Who. By the time they were nearly done decorating, they were laughing and applauding each other's creativity.

"Well," Charlotte said as she looked over their cookie

collection, "this is the most unorthodox batch of Christmas cookies I have ever seen."

"They all taste the same to me," Bill said as he munched on an Aquaman sugar cookie. He smiled, "Delicious!"

"I think we have created a new Christmas Eve tradition," Davis declared. He held up his snowman cookie that he'd decorated to look like a monkey, "The non-traditional cookie tradition."

"After all this sugar, I'm up for a little outdoor adventure," Denny suggested.

"The sleigh isn't quite ready, is it Bill?" Davis asked.

Charlotte perked up, she'd almost forgotten about the sleigh ride.

Bill nodded into his coffee mug, "Not quite, it will be ship shape tomorrow for the Christmas ride."

"Won't that be lovely?" Vicky asked, giving Denny a sweet smile. They were a romantic couple.

"Well, we could snowshoe to Crystal Lake," Davis suggested.

"That sounds great," Denny agreed.

Though far less excited about snowshoeing than she was about sleigh rides, Charlotte didn't want to be a party pooper. She discreetly asked Bill how far Crystal Lake was from the Inn, just to be sure what she was getting herself into.

"Oh, it's just a hop, skip and a jump from the back door," he answered.

Charlotte donned her jacket and sunglasses, and as she strapped her snowshoes over her boots she hoped Bill's idea of a hop, skip and a jump turned out to be not far at all.

The sunshine was brilliant, reflecting off of the whitened landscape and warming the air more than Charlotte thought would be possible. Davis had explained to her that Colorado weather could go from a freezing blizzard to warm and balmy from day to day during the winter. It looked like they were in for a warm day ahead.

Davis led them around the back of the Inn where the back yard sloped easily down to a wide meadow surrounded by pine trees. They made their way down the slope and to the edge of the meadow. As they walked they kicked up snow and tiny flakes floated into the air, sparkling in the sunlight.

Charlotte asked, "So where exactly is Crystal Lake?"

"You're standing on it," Davis answered.

"You're kidding," Denny said, looking around them at what appeared to be a wide open meadow.

"The lake starts about here and extends to those three big trees that are growing in a row," he pointed to a spot in the distance about a football field away from them.

"Wow, it's pretty big isn't it?" Vicky commented.

"Do you have boats and fishing here in the summer?" Denny asked.

"I have a row boat, and yes we have fishing gear. It's deep enough and crystal clear in the summer so it's great for swimming, too."

Denny nodded, looking around and envisioning the summer activities available to patrons of the Inn.

"I would like to get another rowboat and maybe a couple of paddle boats. I think people would like those. I'd also like to invest in half a dozen mountain bikes that guests could check out to utilize the trails around here," Davis continued, getting more and more excited as he described his plans.

As the others talked, Charlotte took in a deep breath of the clean, cold air. She looked back towards the Inn and imagined it was summer and where she stood was a clear mountain lake. There would be green grass where the snow now covered the ground and the pine trees would still be tall and majestic, with birds and other wildlife living in and around them. Crystal Lake Inn was beautiful in the winter, and she thought it would be just as beautiful in the summer.

Turning back, she watched Davis talking about the home he loved so much. As she did she felt a pang of melancholy, wondering if she would ever return here after this Christmas. Her experience had already been so involving, she felt like she belonged. Davis saw her watching them and his eyes smiled in that way he had that made her feel welcome and wanted. Remarkable, really, considering all of the worry she had caused him. She felt another bout of melancholy. Soon she would be heading home to the charade that was her life and she wondered if it was all worth it. The initial excitement and thrill of being on TV had quickly been replaced with the anxiety over not being found out. Plus she didn't like being inauthentic, basically lying. It wasn't who she really was, or at least not who she wanted to be.

After the walk around the frozen, snow covered lake, they settled into a comfortable afternoon inside by the tree. They played a few card games before Davis went outside to help Bill with the final adjustments they were making on the sleigh for tomorrow. Denny and Vicky decided to watch some black and white Christmas movies in the living room, and Charlotte excused herself to her room. They had already prepared a beef roast that was happily cooking away in the crockpot downstairs, and there was nothing more to do for dinner. Her melancholy feeling was growing and she decided that some time alone might be in order.

Charlotte ran a bath in the claw foot tub. Her room came with a basket that included some fun toiletries and she wondered if pampering herself just a little would improve her mood. She poured a lavender mint bubble bath into the water and lit the vanilla scented candles. The smells mingled with the steam from the hot water and Charlotte breathed them all in. Wonderful.

She slipped into the mounds of scented bubbles, the water almost too warm for comfort, which made it extremely relaxing. The smooth porcelain surface of the tub against her skin, the heat seeping into her muscles, the luxuriousness of the bubbles and the candles, all of it encompassed her and she felt her worries slipping away. She sank down into the water, the tub was so deep it easily covered her whole body up to her neck. Her head rested comfortably on the elegant shaped edge and before long, Charlotte fell asleep.

Muffled thumping woke her and she sat up with a start, sloshing tepid water over the edge of the tub. Gripping the sides she saw that the bubbles were long gone and the candles were sputtering. How long had she been asleep?

The thumping again. It wasn't thumping, it was knocking. A voice, too, she could hear someone saying something. They were knocking on the door of her room.

Charlotte pushed herself out of the bath, water streaming off of her body. She stepped onto the plush bathroom rug and grabbed one of the large towels, wrapping herself quickly. The air was already hitting her naked, wet skin and making her shiver.

She popped her head out of the bathroom door and the knocking came clear as day, accompanied by Davis' voice.

"Charlotte, are you in there?"

She hesitated, should she get dressed? The knock came again. Maybe there was something wrong.

"I'm coming," she said, and opened the door halfway, keeping her towel clad body partially blocked by the door.

"There you are," Davis said. He took in her damp hair, bare shoulders and towel, and something switched in his expression. It was only there for a moment, but when he realized she wasn't totally dressed she felt his eyes lock onto hers with such intensity it took her breath away. Her lips parted and she almost gasped. For a single second she thought he was going to step towards her, into her room. Not that she would have necessarily minded. The attraction between them was palpable.

Davis started to say something then looked down at his feet, his cheeks turning red.

"Is everything okay?" She asked.

He nodded, still looking down. Then he cleared his throat and said, "I was, uh, wondering if you were ready for dinner. To make dinner." He risked a look up, concentrating hard on keeping his eyes directly on hers.

Charlotte bit her lip to keep from giggling, "Sure, yes."

"Sorry, I didn't know you..." he didn't finish, instead he lifted his hand and kind of pointed in her general direction.

"Bathed?" She asked, smiling flirtatiously. She was really feeling her oats, as her mother used to say.

He blushed again and laughed this time, turning his head to look away from her, then turning back. This time the look in his eye did not last for only a second. It held. His mouth was turned up in a sly smile and his eyes, those big soulful eyes, looked deep into hers. Without him speaking a word, she knew exactly what he was thinking and it gave her shivers of a very different kind.

Now it was her turn to blush, starting in her chest, rising up her neck and into her cheeks. She broke her gaze away from his and looked at the floor between them.

A few beats passed, then he spoke, his voice low and course, "I'll get things started. See you down there?"

Charlotte glanced up at him, he was still watching her with that sexy, charming smile. She nodded. She didn't think she could speak, her mouth was dry and her heart was pounding. He walked backwards away from her door as she slowly closed it. Once it was shut, she leaned her forehead against the wood and tried to regain her composure.

She quickly blew her hair dry and swept it up so long

tresses fell down her back while a few shorter pieces framed her face nicely. She slipped on her most comfortable black slacks and a Christmas red V-neck sweater that was made with faux Angora and gave her a nice, soft as a cloud look. A little makeup and a black felt choker with a faux diamond stud in the center and she was ready to join the festivities.

As she closed the door to her room, the butterflies in her stomach were so active it felt like she was on her way to meet a date instead of going to help serve roast beef to a client's investors.

CHAPTER 12

D inner went very well. Wine, candles, a juicy roast beef, roasted potatoes and onions, and Davis standing close at every opportunity, touching her shoulder, her elbow, her back, whenever he could. Charlotte found him magnetic. She leaned towards him when he was nearby, her hand ended up right next to his on the counter or at the table. Every sound he made instantly caught her attention and she would stop what she was doing or saying to listen to him.

He looked so handsome tonight. He wore his standard jeans, but had on a black long sleeved button up shirt that she'd never seen him in before. The black brought out the dark tones of his hair and made his blue eyes vibrant. He hadn't shaved for dinner, but that just meant he had a 5 o'clock shadow, which Charlotte thought was one of the sexiest looks on a man.

When they all moved into the living room to sit by the tree and eat their crazy Christmas cookies, Charlotte sat in the chair next to the hearth where Davis perched with his guitar. Their feet were just inches from each other and by the end of the first song their feet were touching. This small physical connection to him sent a thrill through her, but Charlotte didn't think anyone else even noticed.

As Christmas Eve's went, this one topped the charts. The ambience was unmatched, with their stunning tree, the fireplace and the additional lights and candles placed all over the room. Singing old, beloved Christmas carols along with Davis and Denny playing the guitar was the perfect entertainment. Charlotte felt like she was in a storybook, snowed in at a beautiful old Inn with an amazing, attractive Innkeeper. And the feeling that she belonged, that she didn't have anywhere else in the world to be except right here on this night, in this place, with this man, wrapped her soul with joy.

The evening grew late and their singing dwindled. Davis put on classical Christmas music, which fit the mellow end to their Christmas Eve. Soon, Bill stood up to go.

"I've got a lot of things to do in the morning to get the horses hitched up to that sleigh, so I'm gonna hit the hay," he said. Giving them all a half salute, "Merry Christmas Eve."

"You too, Bill," Vicky said, giving him her brilliant toothy smile.

"See you in the morning," Denny answered. He stretched his arms, disturbing Bernie who was on the couch with his head in Denny's lap, "It's about that time for us, too, isn't it?" He looked at Vicky for confirmation.

"Yes," she agreed. She stroked Blanche who was snoring quietly in her lap, "This has been such a beautiful night, though."

They all agreed and the Foss' made moves to take their empty dishes to the kitchen. Davis told them not to worry about the cups and plates, he would pick them up. Charlotte started gathering up any dishes from the living room and took them into the kitchen. Of course she was stalling to be alone with Davis, but she hoped by staying busy it wouldn't be completely obvious to everyone else.

Davis popped into the kitchen carrying his own stack of dishes. He put them hastily down on the island and grabbed two wine glasses and a half drunk bottle of Merlot off the counter.

"Come with me?" He asked, grinning and holding out his hand to her. She took it, no questions asked.

Davis leaned through the door that led from the kitchen to the living room and looked around.

"Coast is clear," he said to her. She giggled and let him pull her gently to the couch where he sat her down before easing down right next to her, their bodies touching, their legs relaxed against each other's. "Wine?" He asked as he poured Merlot into each glass.

"Yes, thank you," she answered, though she doubted wine could add anything to the warm glow she was already feeling.

He handed her a glass, then settled back with his own. His torso was turned towards her and one arm rested casually on the couch behind her head.

"Cheers," he said.

They clinked glasses.

"Cheers," she answered, though her voice was barely audible.

Charlotte swallowed some wine and tried to keep her free hand from wandering up and touching the 5 o'clock shadow on his face. At any moment something was going to happen between them, that was clear. She'd never been so certain of a physical attraction. Perhaps the wine would allow it to happen smoothly with no embarrassing hiccups.

Davis placed his wine glass on the coffee table and turned to her, "Do you remember when we were talking about having...chemistry?"

She cocked her eyebrow at him, "When you were talking about us having chemistry?"

"Yes," he glanced down then back up, a grin on his face, "when I was talking about us having chemistry."

She nodded, "Yes, I remember."

"I think...I feel like that chemistry has just gotten stronger since then," he waited for her to respond.

"I agree," she said, then took an innocent sip of her wine.

Davis slid his hand onto her knee and let his thumb caress the sensitive skin on the inside of her leg. She took another sip of her wine, then put her glass down on the coffee table so she could lay her hand over his.

"But didn't you say something about us not getting involved?" She asked coyly.

"Yes, I did," he admitted.

"So what's changed?"

"What's changed?

She nodded. He gave a short laugh that was almost a scoff, but when she watched him evenly waiting for an answer, he stopped laughing.

"Okay, okay," he took a few seconds to look away and gather his thoughts. When he looked back at her he had that same intense gaze that had pushed her over the edge when she was in her towel, "Charlotte, these past few days have been...they've been great. It's been so much fun doing things with you, cooking with you, planning with you. I've...I've always felt alone here. Not always lonely, that would be sad, but kind of alone in my love for this place, and living and working here. Even when I was married, I think I still felt alone." He lifted his hand that was resting on the couch and touched her hair with his fingertips, his eyes tracing the shape of her face. Charlotte melted.

"That's so sad," she whispered.

He shifted his gaze to her and smiled shyly, "Maybe it is.

But I haven't felt that way since you've been here, since we've been, you know, cooking together."

She gave a little laugh, but her eyes were tearing up with the emotion of it all.

"Don't cry," he said, moving his fingers from her hair to her cheek to wipe away the single tear that had escaped. "It's been fun. I think you've been having fun, too?" He waited for her to respond. She nodded, sniffling. "I never thought I would ever feel so...connected to anyone. I never thought someone so funny, and kind, and beautiful, and sexy would be here with me, and yet here you are," he let his fingers trace her cheek until they reached her mouth, then he ran his thumb lightly over her bottom lip, making it tickle.

Charlotte moved her hand from where it rested on his, and ran it up his forearm then his bicep, feeling the muscles flex as she did. As her hand slipped over the top of his arm and along his broad, strong shoulder, he leaned towards her, dipping his head down to hers, catching her mouth with his.

The heat and pressure of his lips betrayed his desire even as he moved his hand back to play softly with her hair. He was so gentle, but she could feel his controlled passion trembling just under the surface. Charlotte's fingers slid from his shoulder and around his neck then up, up into that thick mop of dark, wavy hair that she'd wanted to touch for days. Davis moved his hand from her knee, up her thigh and to her waist, wrapping his arm firmly around her and pulling her to him. She went willingly. She was falling fast and hard under his charms, an eager captive in his arms and the whole world spun away.

They stayed bound together on the couch long into the night. Sharing kisses, memories, laughter, hopes and fears, as the hour grew later and later. Davis stoked the fire some more, they drank another glass of wine, he pulled two blankets out of a nearby cupboard and had her snuggle with him under them to stay warm and comfy. They couldn't bring themselves to leave the fire and the Christmas tree, afraid maybe that the magic would be broken if they stepped out of the room.

Charlotte fought the urge to pinch herself. She was floating on cloud nine, head over heels, and a hundred other clichés about falling in love. Being with Davis had always been easy, being physical like this with him felt so natural it was like they had been together forever. She felt no awkwardness or anxiety, just joy and an excellent zip of excitement. She couldn't stop herself from touching him and reveled in the way it felt when he moved his hands over her or wrapped her up in his arms. Finally they lay together on the couch, his head on the armrest and her head on his chest.

"I feel really awful," he told her as she listened to his heartbeat and the deep rumble of his voice.

"For what?"

"I don't have a Christmas present for you," he confessed. He held a strand of her hair and was winding it up and down his finger.

"You beast!" She lifted her head up and gave him a mock scowl, "How could you?"

"I know!" He answered, chuckling.

"That's okay," she said lightly. She lifted her face to his and he bent down, allowing her to kiss him on the tip of his nose, "I didn't get you anything either."

"Hmm," he acted disappointed. Then he smiled and snuggled deeper into the couch to make sure she was comfortable, "There's always next year."

"Yeah, next year," she said happily.

Shortly after, they fell asleep.

CHAPTER 13

When Charlotte woke up the fire had turned to ash. The Christmas tree lights were still glowing and it was still dark outside. She was curled up on the worn leather couch covered in the blankets Davis had gotten for them, but she was alone. Davis was nowhere in sight.

Charlotte sat up, wondering what time it was. A look out the window told her it was not yet dawn. She was sleepy and as the blankets fell away she felt a biting chill on her shoulders. She pulled them up and over her again, leaned back on the couch, and thought about Davis.

She could still feel his warmth, his sweet kisses and gentle touch still glowed on her skin. The more she thought about him the more her heart swelled in her chest. The joy in her body and soul over this wonderful, funny, adorable man whose arms she'd fallen asleep in last night was almost overwhelming. Thinking about him woke her up and she decided to make some coffee while she waited for him to come back from wherever he had gone.

Her hair a mess, askew from sleeping on it, and wrapped

in one of the blankets to fend off the cold, Charlotte padded in her stocking feet to the kitchen. She didn't turn on the light because the moon shone bright enough through the window for her to see. Turning on the lights seemed too garish in the hushed silence of the old Inn.

She opened the fridge and a stream of light poured over her into the kitchen. Squinting to see in the sudden brightness, she grabbed the half and half from a shelf in the door and closed the fridge quickly. As she opened the cupboard above the coffee pot and plucked out the tin of coffee and the sugar bowl, she thought she saw something out of the corner of her eye, a movement just past the window. She placed the items on the counter and closed the cupboard then shuffled over to peer out of the window at the drifting snow lit in blue moonlight.

The moon was big and bright in the deep black night. It illuminated the shapes of the pine trees in the near distance, and reflected off of the snow-covered ground, giving the scene even more light. As her eyes adjusted she thought she saw two objects, what looked like two people, standing very still in the snow a short distance from the house. A stab of fear shot through her stomach and she started to step back into the shadows of the kitchen when another form, this one dark like a shadow, and definitely moving, popped into view just outside the window.

Charlotte screamed, stumbling backwards into a kitchen chair in her fright. The figure hit the window with a flat palm and Charlotte screamed again. A muffled male voice came to her and she could just make out the words he was saying.

"It's me! It's me," he hit the window with his palm again and suddenly Charlotte recognized Davis. He had on his jacket, a wool hat, ski gloves and a scarf wrapped around his neck and mouth.

She walked up to the window, pulling the blanket tighter

around her shoulders, half laughing and half scolding him for giving her such a fright.

"What are you doing out there?" Her breath fogged up the window.

"Mwoo ashy," Davis said.

She giggled, "I can't understand you."

He leaned closer to the glass and so did she, putting her fingertips against the icy smooth surface. Davis put his hand against hers on the other side. She could barely see his eyes under all of his bundling. He pulled his scarf down so his mouth was exposed.

"Come outside," he said again.

He met her at the red front door. He had a layer of snow caked on his legs and arms, like he'd been crawling through the drifts. A wall of bitter cold took her breath away when she opened the door.

"Do you want your jacket? It's pretty cold," his words floated like fog in the freezing air.

She plopped her red hat on top of her head, slipped her boots over her feet and shook her head 'no', "This blanket is warm enough."

She made sure the blanket was hanging evenly around her body and pulled tight around her shoulders and waist, then Davis put his hand on the small of her back and guided her around to the back of the house. The moon was even more massive when seen from outside. It hung in the sky like a great globe that seemed close enough to touch. He stopped her when they were in the back yard and pointed to a spot outside the kitchen window where two snowmen stood side by side.

"It's us!" Davis said proudly.

"Us?" She took another look. One snow figure was tall and one was short, and they were standing very close to each other, so close their stick arms looked like they were touching, "Are they holding hands?"

"Yep," Davis said, clapping his hands together to keep them warm.

Charlotte laughed, "You're crazy!"

"You said you thought there should be snowmen out here."

"I did, you're right," she had to agree.

"And since I didn't get you a Christmas present..."

"You came out and built these in the middle of the night?"

"It's almost morning, actually, so not exactly the middle of the night," he grinned at her.

"That is so sweet," Charlotte beamed at him.

"Merry Christmas, Charlotte," Davis said, leaning down to kiss her on the lips then once on the tip of her nose.

"Merry Christmas," she answered. The cold was seeping through her blanket and she shivered, "Now let's go inside. It's freezing out here!"

They warmed themselves with fresh coffee and watched the pink light of dawn appear in the night sky. The snow people went from vague forms in the moonlight to round, happy looking snow friends holding hands and waving into the kitchen window with their stick arms. When it was light enough, Davis ran back outside and stuck carrot noses in their faces. He also pulled two scarves out of his jacket that he must have retrieved from the foyer somewhere, one was red and one was green. He waved them at Charlotte before wrapping the red scarf on what was supposed to be her and the green one on the taller snowman that was supposed to be him.

Soon the others would be waking up, so they decided to shower and get dressed for the day then meet back in the kitchen to cook breakfast. There were big plans in the works to make omelets.

Davis made it back to the kitchen before Charlotte. The crooning of Michael Buble Christmas music drifted to her as she came down the stairs. Pausing before she walked into the kitchen, she took a moment to look at Davis through the doorway and let herself swoon a little bit. He had on black jeans and a dark red sweater pulled over a white, collared shirt. His hair was still damp, making the wave in it even more pronounced. He was freshly shaved and stood at the island concentrating on slicing green onions. He whistled along with the music as he worked, and Charlotte could have stayed there forever just watching him.

Michael started the next song, *Have Yourself a Merry Little Christmas*, and as Davis sang the line he glanced up and saw her. She looked down, feeling shy, caught admiring him from afar. He put down his knife and continued singing as he waltz walked towards her, an impossibly adorable look of fun on his face.

Davis took her waist and slid his free hand into hers. He kept singing along with the music, his deep voice rivaling Buble's in sexiness, as he twirled her slowly across the tile floor. It felt good to be in his arms again, so natural, so comforting. She gazed up at him, full of joy and contentment and, dare she even think it? Love?

Could she be falling in love with Davis?

Every time he touched her or looked at her she was filled with a rush of happiness. When she touched him or looked at him, or even simply thought about him, it was like everything else in the world fell away. She allowed the idea to linger. A deep sense of connection blossomed from her core and permeated every part of her as they danced. His eyes were sparkling with fun like always, and with something more. It was as if he was looking deep into her soul, seeing what she was feeling and connecting to it, feeling it himself.

He slowed their twirling until they were stopped. The

music surrounded them, morning sun shone brilliant through the kitchen windows. Davis wasn't singing anymore. He searched her eyes for an answer to the unasked question between them. They wanted each other, that was certain, but could they be...were they in love? Charlotte felt his breathing increase, hers did too. His arm tightened around her waist.

"Charlotte," he said.

She moved her hand from where it was resting lightly on his shoulder to his cheek. She felt him relax at her touch and melt into her a little more. She wanted to kiss him so she turned her mouth up towards him.

"Charlotte," he said again, his voice hoarse with emotion as he leaned down.

"Charlie?!" A woman's voice broke into their moment and Charlotte jumped at the sound. Davis released her and they instantly pulled away from each other, looking towards the sound.

"Bella!" Charlotte almost shouted.

Bella had finally arrived.

CHAPTER 14

Bella stood in the doorway to the kitchen, mouth agape, hands on hips. She was a tiny woman, very thin with long, curly caramel colored hair and gigantic brown eyes that seemed even bigger at the shock of finding Charlotte in the arms of a man.

"Bella, you made it!" Charlotte exclaimed. She knew her face was flushed with embarrassment. Hurrying over to Bella, she leaned in to give her a hug.

"What are you doing?" Bella whispered into her ear as they hugged.

"I'll tell you later," Charlotte whispered back, then separated and threw her arm towards Davis, who was leaning casually against the other side of the island watching her with an amused, if slightly chagrined, expression. "This is Davis Reed, the owner of the Inn," Charlotte announced.

Bella gave her a quick wide-eyed look of surprise, then smiled gracefully at Davis, "Of course, Mr. Reed, very nice to meet you."

He gave Bella a nod, "It's good to meet you."

"Sorry I'm late," Bella's smile was part grimace. Davis

laughed a little at her joke. His face, too, was slightly red from being caught in the middle of a kiss.

He cleared his throat, "The roads are open?"

"Barely open. It was quite a drive from the hotel, but I left early." Bella shifted her eyes from him back to Charlotte, then to the green onions left half chopped on the wood cutting board and the carton of eggs next to the stove. "You haven't made breakfast already, have you?" She asked, taking off the winter coat she still wore.

"No," Davis and Charlotte answered at the same time.

"We—uh, we were going to make omelets?" He turned his statement into a question at the last moment.

"I see," Bella said.

The expression on Bella's face made Charlotte feel like an intruder in the kitchen. It must have done the same to Davis, because he seemed to make a decision and approached them, reaching for Bella's coat.

"Let me take your coat and maybe..." he looked at Charlotte for help.

"Bella and I will make breakfast," she said.

She was having a flash of professional guilt. She'd almost forgotten that Davis had hired them, that this was a business deal. There was no reason for Davis to cook when he had brought them in to do the cooking and Bella was actually here to do it right.

"Oh...okay," Davis looked confused and a little disappointed. Charlotte gave him a small smile as Bella handed over her coat. He nodded, understanding that maybe he should step out of the room, "I'll leave you to it."

"Breakfast will be ready in an hour," Bella told him in her commanding chef voice.

As soon as he left, she whirled around to face Charlotte.

"Charlie, what are you doing with the Innkeeper?" It was both a scolding and a girlfriend's request for gossip.

Charlotte lowered her eyes, trying to keep from gushing like a schoolgirl, "We've gotten kind of...close."

"Close?" Bella threw her hands in the air, "I think he was about to kiss you! That's more than close," she narrowed her eyes at Charlotte, suspicious that her friend was not giving her all of the information.

"Should I give you a tour of the kitchen?" Charlotte offered a distraction.

Bella shook her head in mild frustration, "I know a kitchen. Any kitchen. Kitchens are no stranger to me."

Charlotte smiled, Bella had a tendency to go on little rants and she heard one coming on.

Bella stomped to the nearest cupboard and opened it, quickly looking at its contents while she fumed, "I'm driving and driving for days, through blizzards! And she," Bella shut the cupboard door, used her thumb to indicate Charlotte, then opened the next cupboard door for inspection. "She is dancing around kitchens getting kissed by handsome men!"

And so it went, Bella slammed around the kitchen absorbing all of the resources available, all the while going off about the shenanigans that had happened while she wasn't here. Charlotte listened and tried not to laugh. Yes, it had been embarrassing to be walked in on and, yes, maybe her budding romance with Davis was unprofessional, but nothing could dim the spark she'd felt with him this morning. She was looking at the world through a prism of love, which made everything seem like a rainbow.

When Bella had gone through all of the cupboards, drawers, and the refrigerator she stopped. Turning towards Charlotte she put her hands on her hips again, waiting for a response.

Charlotte didn't blink, "Do you know what you want to make for breakfast?"

Bella smiled, waving her hand over her head as if erasing

all of the words she'd just said. "Ah, well, such is life. Let's get busy!"

In one hour they had a spread on the table that would impress anyone. It was like Bella's cooking instincts had been suppressed for days and now that they were released had blown up all over the table. There was a hot chocolate bar with real whipped cream and dark chocolate shavings to sprinkle on top, vanilla cranberry mimosas, ricotta rosemary and tomato mini quiches, herb biscuit sandwiches made with maple sage pork sausage, a stack of hickory smoked bacon, and blueberry pancakes shaped like little gingerbread men, complete with fat, fresh blueberries for their eyes and buttons.

Bella stood back to look at the table bursting with goodies, her eyes shining.

"It looks delicious, Bella," Charlotte said.

Bella took her hand and squeezed it, "I'm sorry I left you on your own here."

Charlotte squeezed back, "It all worked out fine. I'm just glad you made it, this is gorgeous!" She was excited for Davis and the others to see it. What a wonderful Christmas Day breakfast.

The familiar clickety clacking of little nails trotting down the hallway towards the kitchen diverted Bella's attention. Charlotte didn't have time to explain before the Biddlebumps rounded the corner. Bella's eyes flew open and she squealed with delight.

"Oh my goodness, who has these puppies?" She dropped to her knees and held out her arms. The Biddlebumps, who could sense when a human was about to adore them, sped up and ran as fast as their fat little rumps would let them into Bella's waiting embrace. "Hello, amorcitos!" She exclaimed.

Denny and Vicky arrived soon after and the introductions

began. When Bill and Davis came in for breakfast, the mood was light and cheery, just like a Christmas morning should be.

Though Bella's arrival had pulled Charlotte and Davis away from each other and put them firmly back into a chef/client relationship, at least on the surface, she still caught him watching her throughout breakfast. Whenever they shared a look, however brief, a thrill shimmered through her body and she wished she could devise some way of being alone with him again.

That chance came about mid-morning when she and Bella were in the throes of preparation for the elaborate feast Bella was planning for Christmas dinner.

Davis popped his head in the kitchen, "Excuse me, ladies."

They both turned towards him. He stood awkwardly, his hands shoved into his pockets, looking a little like a teenager asking a girl out on a date.

"We are going to take the sleigh out for a test run," his eyes hung on Charlotte, "Would you like to come with me? I did promise you would have the first ride."

Would she like to go for a sleigh ride? Of course she would! She was about to say 'yes', then stopped herself, worried about leaving Bella with all of the work. She looked at her friend, who was shifting her eyes back and forth between the two lovebirds. Then, suddenly, Bella threw her hands up in the air.

"Of course she wants to go on the sleigh," Bella exclaimed, shaking her head that he would even have to ask.

"Will you be okay here without me?" Charlotte asked.

"Me? Of course!" Bella pooh poohed Charlotte's concern, "Come back when you're done so you can do something wonderful with the table."

Charlotte agreed and within a few minutes she and Davis were bundled up and walking to the barn. He took her gloved hand in his as discreetly as possible. She loved how it felt, sweet and strong.

He gave her a grin, "I like her."

"Yeah, she's pretty great."

The sound of the front door opening made them turn. They saw Bella hurrying towards them, the Biddlebumps close on her heels.

"Wait!" Bella said. She walked carefully, but swiftly, over the packed snow carrying a brown paper bag. When she reached them she pushed the bag at Charlotte, "You can't have a sleigh ride without hot chocolate!"

Inside the bag she'd packed a thermos full of hot chocolate, mugs, a plastic container full of marshmallows, and gingerbread men from their pile of decorated cookies. Bella really did know how to throw a party.

Davis led Charlotte to the far side of the barn that wasn't visible from the house. When they turned the corner Charlotte was speechless at the sight of two beautiful bay horses with glossy coats, red ribbons braided into their black manes and a string of sleigh bells hanging over each of their necks. Bill was holding the horses and they were hitched to the sleigh, an honest to goodness red sleigh, like something out of a storybook. Charlotte's face must have shown her excitement, because Davis and Bill shared a look of satisfaction.

"You're going on the first ride, Miss Charlotte?" Bill asked.

She nodded. She couldn't speak. It was all too wonderful. She took off her glove and ran her hand over the noses of each of the bays. Whenever they moved there was a light tingle of noise from the bells. Then Davis showed her the ornate black iron step used to climb in, and she marveled at the plush black velvet bench seats, running her hand along the shining red curves of the body of the sleigh.

"Where did you get this?" Charlotte wondered, amazed at

the fluid shape of the wood and the way the runners circled up high in the front, giving it an old fashioned feeling.

"My Dad built it," Davis said, pleased at her response. He held the hot chocolate bag and offered her his hand so she could step in. There were two sets of seats facing each other, so the sleigh could seat four people. She sat in the seat facing front.

"Really? That's so impressive, this is absolutely beautiful," she exclaimed.

"Samuel Reed was a master builder," Bill said, not without some emotion.

"Samuel was your Dad's name?" She asked.

Davis nodded and climbed in, sitting next to her. He grabbed a heavy red and black plaid wool blanket from the other seat and spread it over their laps.

"Ready for the maiden run?" Bill asked.

"Yes, sir," Davis answered. He looked to her and she nodded happily. Happy didn't quite capture how she felt. Blissful. Gleeful. Merry! That was it, she truly felt merry on Christmas Day.

Bill climbed into the driver's seat and clicked his tongue at the horses. They started to walk and the sleigh pulled away from the barn and along the fence towards the woods. The sleigh bells jingled steadily and Charlotte was in seventh heaven. Davis found her hand under the blanket, taking it in his.

They slid smoothly across the bright, sparkling meadows and through the towering snow covered pine trees. The sun warmed their faces, but Charlotte was glad to have the blanket and Davis next to her to keep her cozy. Being carried along was easier than snowshoeing, but sitting so still did not allow the body to warm up from exercise.

She snuggled closer to Davis and he leaned down, kissing her on her forehead.

"Are you warm enough?" He asked.

"Yes, as long as you stay next to me."

He adjusted so one arm was over her shoulder, pulling her closer to his chest. The other hand held hers under the blanket. Cuddled into him, she enjoyed the beautiful landscape. The quiet of the woods was broken only by the jingling sleigh bells and the occasional sound of clumps of snow dropping from the tops of the trees where the sun softened them, letting them slide off the branches.

When they were deep in the woods, Davis broke open the hot chocolate and they carefully poured the steaming drink into two mugs. Bless Bella, she'd remembered to provide a mug for Bill, too. He declined any refreshment for now, saying he would have some when they were back at the barn. Charlotte plopped fat marshmallows on top of the hot chocolate in two of the mugs and she and Davis settled back under the blanket to enjoy their treat.

"Are you having fun?" Davis asked.

"Am I having fun?" Charlotte returned his question. She looked around at the scenery then back at Davis, "I'm drinking hot chocolate on a sleigh ride through the woods on Christmas Day..." she left off the last part of the sentence that she would have said if Bill had been out of earshot, 'with you'. She squeezed his hand under the covers and hoped that he knew what she meant. He did.

Davis glanced at Bill's back, making sure the older man wouldn't see what he was about to do. A mischievous look entered his eyes, and he leaned in to kiss Charlotte full on the mouth. Charlotte was sure she had never had as perfect a Christmas Day as this one.

Suddenly, she was struck with a brilliant decorating idea for the Christmas Dinner table. It would be elegant, fairly simple to create, and something totally unique. Honestly, she didn't think this day could get any better.

CHAPTER 15

Charlotte and Bella spent the rest of the morning and early afternoon in the kitchen. Bella did most of the cooking, obviously, while Charlotte sat at the table and made elaborate paper snowflakes, part of her idea for the Christmas dinner decorations.

Bella hadn't pried about the sleigh ride after they returned. She was too busy cooking, which was fine with Charlotte. She and Davis were in that tender beginning phase of a romance, the time when it didn't feel right to show it to the outside world yet. They needed time to let it grow in private before they knew for sure what it was, to be certain the fantasy was going to stick and become reality.

When Davis and Bill came in from taking care of the horses, Davis offered to help in the kitchen. Bella told him in a very polite way that they had everything under control.

"No, thank you so very much. No need. Since I'm here now, I think we are fine on our own," Bella looked at Charlotte to agree.

There was an awkward pause. She and Davis had grown used to the time they spent in the kitchen together. It had become a comfortable, homey space for them both. Their private place. Their little secret. With Bella there the reality of it being a working kitchen at a professional establishment felt like a giant wedge being shoved between them. Charlotte smiled apologetically at him, hoping he wasn't offended.

"You should relax for a while," she suggested. "Would you like something to drink?" She heard the tone in her voice yet couldn't stop it. She sounded like a hostess, or a chef, or the star of the show. What she didn't sound like was someone who had spent all last night and half the morning cuddled in his arms.

A look of confusion passed through his eyes. His gaze flicked to Bella cooking at the stove then back to Charlotte. He started to say something, then shook it off and instead hovered a little pitifully in the hallway like a child who's been sent to his room.

"I can get my own drink," he said under his breath.

"I know, I didn't mean it that way," she answered. "I mean we've got this, don't we Bella?"

Bella lifted the long metal spatula she'd been using to sauté a pan of onions into the air over her head in a kind of salute.

"Okay, okay," he conceded.

"Maybe you can visit with Denny and Vicky? Make sure they're okay?" Charlotte suggested.

He looked down the hallway towards the living room then back at her, his hair tumbling into his eyes in his particular irresistible style. He reached one hand discreetly towards her stomach, took the fabric of her shirt between his thumb and forefinger and tugged lightly. The move was intimate, tantalizing.

"See you in a little bit?" He asked, his voice deep and low.

"Of course," she answered, his touch sending a thrill across her skin.

She didn't see him for almost an hour and a half. Not until she brought trays of hors d'oeuvres into the living room to put out on the coffee table for everyone to share. Bella had whipped up cranberry Brie bites, prosciutto wrapped asparagus and cheddar crab puffs to hold everyone over until dinner.

"These smell great," Denny said, taking two of each.

"Thank you, Charlotte," Vicky added. "And I don't just mean for the hors d'oeuvres," Vicky gave Charlotte a shoulder hug and pointed under the Christmas tree. There was a pile of crumpled wrapping paper next to the vintage light bulb wreath she had helped Denny make. "I love it! It's so kitschy," Vicky giggled and Charlotte laughed with her, glad the gift had gone over well.

Denny gave Charlotte a wink and a nod, adding, "She really loves it."

"I'm so glad. Denny did all of the hard work," Charlotte responded.

Betting that his owners were distracted by conversation, Bernie Biddlebump made a move for the hors d'oeuvres. He put his front paws up on the edge of the coffee table and strained to reach one of the trays, but his little fat neck was not terribly stretchy and he only managed to lick the edge of the dish.

"Bernie, get down," Vicky scolded, but her voice was not angry. She didn't get angry with anyone, least of all her Pugs.

Blanche, seeing Bernie's antics, decided she deserved whatever goodies he was getting into on the coffee table. Fortunately for them, unfortunately for her, Blanche's little body wasn't quite as nubile as Bernie's and she couldn't stand up next to him at all. Instead she hopped around breathing hard and whining.

"Now look, you're getting Blanche in a tizzy," Vicky said to Bernie. He looked up at her with his bulging eyes and wrinkled black face and gave her a sneeze, a clear sign he was asking for a treat.

"Aww, are you hungry, Bernie?" Charlotte leaned down and pet the little dog's head. "Why don't I take them to the kitchen and find them something more dog friendly?"

"Oh, would you?" Vicky sighed happily, "They've been vexing me all morning getting into things." Vicky and Denny had also been partaking heavily in Bill's special 'Jingle Juice' punch and probably needed a break, maybe even a nap, before dinner.

"I'll help you," Davis offered, scooping Bernie up in his arms. The little dog waggled his non-existent tail enthusiastically, "C'mon Bernie."

Charlotte picked Blanche up in her arms and joined Davis in the hallway. Halfway to the kitchen, Davis stopped. She stopped, too. He made sure the coast was clear then stole a kiss. She blushed, checking up and down the hallway in case he'd missed a possible witness.

"What are you doing, Mr. Reed?" She whispered.

Davis pointed to the ceiling and Charlotte looked up to see mistletoe hanging from the light fixture above them. When she looked back down he stole another kiss.

"That is exactly how mistletoe is supposed to work," he said with delight. He chuckled at her expression, which was a mixture of surprise and amusement. "Now, Bernie," he spoke to the snuffling little dog in his arms, "I don't want to hear a peep out of you about this to anyone." Bernie responded by trying to lick Davis' chin.

Once back in the kitchen, and after the Biddlebumps were properly fed, both Charlotte and Davis were pulled into the frenzied fun of putting together an amazing Christmas dinner. Bella was more open to Davis assisting than she had been earlier, mostly because the whole event was coming to a head and she needed as many hands as possible to complete it to her satisfaction.

They helped her chop and stir and sauté and spice until everything was comfortably roasting or bubbling or resting on the island to put on the table later. Then Davis helped Charlotte finish her Christmas dinner decorations, which she affectionately labeled 'Let it Snow'.

They draped some extra strings of white lights all over the rustic chandelier that hung over the kitchen table. Then they hung the delicate paper snowflakes and stars Charlotte had made earlier so that they dangled over the table at varying lengths. They laid out the white china with the silver pattern around the edge that almost looked like fine lace. For the center of the table Charlotte used a white lace runner. On the runner she placed a half dozen tabletop white reindeer statues she'd found in Davis' Christmas decoration boxes, arranging them into two groups of threes.

The reindeer were old and their faces were a 1950's style, but their fur was still pure white and soft and they looked sweet placed around the silver candlesticks with long white candles reaching towards the snowflakes. She used the all white linen napkins with antique silver napkin rings she'd found in the china cabinet. With the best crystal wine glasses and the silverware laid out, the table had a glimmering, fanciful look to it. Charlotte was pleased, as were Bella and Davis.

"Stunning, Charlie," Bella exclaimed. "And there are places for the Biddlebumps," she noticed.

"We couldn't leave the Biddlebumps on the floor for Christmas dinner," Davis said. He looked proudly at Charlotte, "Especially when it's going to be such an amazing Christmas dinner."

It was true. They had set two places for the Pugs and Charlotte drew up place cards with their names on them as well as all of the human guests. Davis kept some old card stock in his office and all Charlotte needed for place cards was a pair of scissors and a black gel pen. As he watched her write each person's name in even cursive then embellish the card with small decorative borders, Davis was impressed.

"You really make pretty things," he said, admiring the card with his name. Then he looked at her thoughtfully.

"What?"

"You know you're beautiful," it wasn't a question, just a statement. It wasn't even said with any desire to hold her hand or kiss her or anything like that. He simply said it, believed it, and wanted her to know that he did.

When Christmas dinner was ready they all gathered around the table full of delicious food and held hands. It was Denny's idea, but they all agreed it felt right. Of course the Biddlebumps merely waited in their makeshift booster seats that Davis had put together using boxes full of old papers and topped off with a pillow, just high enough for them to be at the table, but with the sides of the box keeping them from sliding off. The rest of them held hands and Denny asked Bill if he would say some kind of grace. Bill obliged with a short disclaimer in the beginning.

"I'm happy to say grace," Bill said. "I'm afraid I'm not much of a praying man, but I do know some Christmas carols that I've been singing since I was a boy. So here goes," he bowed his head and they all followed suit. "Little town of Bethlehem, how still we see thee lie. Above thy deep and dreamless sleep the silent stars go by. Yet in thy dark streets shineth the everlasting Light. The hopes and fears of all the years are met in thee tonight. Amen."

It was completely simple and utterly perfect. Davis squeezed her hand and when she looked at him she was teary eyed. She couldn't help it. He lifted one side of his mouth in a crooked, comforting smile then they all sat down to eat.

"You have really outdone yourself today, Charlotte," Vicky said as she took a bite of sweet potato soufflé.

Charlotte looked quickly at Bella who, to her credit, took the comment in stride. She always did. They had never clashed over the fact that Charlotte got all of the credit while Bella did all of the work.

"Here, here," Denny agreed. He pointed at the stuffed turkey breast on his plate, "This is the juiciest turkey I've ever eaten in my life."

"Well," Charlotte looked down at her lap, ashamed at the praise.

"Well done," Davis added, lifting his wine glass to her in a toast. Her eyes fixed on him, shocked that he was going along with the charade and leaving Bella out when he knew the truth. Then he shifted his attention to Bella and raised his glass to her as well, "And to Bella, for coming along just in time."

"Yes," Charlotte added quickly, relieved at his inclusion of the real chef. "Without Bella we wouldn't be enjoying such a wonderful dinner," she raised her glass at Bella who played the part of the humble assistant.

"Here, here," Denny said to Bella, and they all clinked glasses and drank.

Dinner was wonderful. They ate their fill, laughing and drinking and generally enjoying themselves. The Biddle-bumps sat in their booster boxes excitedly gobbling up any small morsels that were placed in front of them.

The afternoon sun was beginning to wane. They'd started dinner a little bit early to ensure Denny and Vicky had a sleigh ride before dark fell. All was moving along as planned and Charlotte sensed how pleased and relaxed Davis was about everything. She didn't know if he'd spoken to Denny and Vicky about any specifics, but she got the feeling Davis was pretty confident they were planning on investing. She hoped this was true and that his financial troubles were behind him. She also hoped at least part of his good mood was due to her.

He caught her eye and held it, giving her the sweetest look. Surely everyone at the table would know their secret if he kept gazing at her like this, but she couldn't look away. Suddenly, a sound from the hallway broke his focus and Davis looked towards the entrance to the kitchen.

"What's tha–?" He started to say, then paused. The sound became clearer. Footsteps. High heels of some kind clicking briskly down the hall towards them. They all stopped talking and listened. Charlotte looked towards the door then back to Davis. All the sweetness had drained from his face. What remained looked stiff, almost sick to his stomach, and something else...protective?

Davis stood up from his chair just as the high heels rounded the corner into the kitchen and stopped. Everyone at the table stared at the woman standing in the doorway. Blanche Biddlebump let out a tiny, continuous growl.

The woman was tall and slender with curves in all of the best places. Her perfectly straightened strawberry blonde hair framed fair skin and high cheekbones, before falling gracefully over her shoulders. Her green-blue eyes were wide set, large and slightly almond shaped. Combined with her full lips, elegant neck and what appeared to be perfectly formed breasts under her form fitting silver and white sweater, she looked like a model.

"Sam," Davis said, his voice sounded tight and uncomfortable.

"Davis," she responded in a cool smooth tone.

"What are you doing here?" He asked.

Her lips split into a smile, revealing dazzling straight, white teeth, "I've come for Christmas dinner."

CHAPTER 16

Though Davis had never used her first name in conversation, Charlotte instantly knew Sam was his ex-wife by the tone in his voice and the proprietary way she breezed into the kitchen. Davis tensed and shifted his eyes quickly to Charlotte before stepping towards Sam in an awkward attempt to block her.

It didn't work. She blithely stepped around him and came straight to the table. Denny and Bill both stood. She was that kind of woman, the kind that men stood for when she approached them. None of them could keep their eyes off of her. Though Blanche was still growling.

"Blanche, that's enough," Vicky said, putting her hand on the Pug's head to silence her.

Sam took in the Biddlebumps sitting at the table with little amusement. None, in fact. Her eyes flicked from the Pugs to the messy dishes on the table to the paper snowflakes hanging from the chandelier, passed over Bill and landed on Denny. Her smile widened and the perfect whiteness of her teeth must have put Denny over the edge.

"Hello," Denny stuck out his hand. Sam took it lightly.

"I'm Denny Foss, this is my wife..." Denny seemed to forget Vicky's name. Confusion clouded his eyes.

Vicky looked at Charlotte and almost rolled her eyes, then she smiled politely at Sam and said, "Vicky, I'm Vicky Foss."

"Wonderful to meet you," Sam's cool voice was smooth. "I'm so glad you made it for the holiday. I wasn't sure with all of this snow," Sam continued.

"Right," Denny agreed heartily. "It was quite an adventure getting here," his enthusiasm on the subject waned when Vicky put a hand on his arm. He looked down at her and started to sit, brought back to earth by his lovely wife. A thought struck him and he stood back up, "Would you like to have a seat?"

Charlotte glanced around. The table sat eight and all of those seats were taken. Denny seemed to come to that realization at the same moment she did. He fumbled, offering to move one of the Biddlebumps so Sam could sit down. It was all getting rather awkward and Davis simply stood, frozen halfway between the doorway and the table, watching Sam interrupt their perfect dinner.

"Have my place," Bill interrupted. He stood up and pushed his chair back.

"Thank you, Bill," Sam said without looking at him.

Charlotte and Bella shared a raised eyebrow. They agreed with unspoken communication, they didn't like her.

Sam sat down in Bill's chair and directed her wide green-blue eyes at Charlotte, "And you're Chef Charlotte." She said it with what must have been meant as pleasure, but Charlotte's hackles went up at the sound of the words. Condescending. That was how everything Sam did came across.

"Yes, I am," Charlotte attempted to smile, but it kind of blurted out of her mouth. Not smooth. Not smooth at all.

"So glad to have you here," Sam said.

Why did she keep talking like she was the proprietor of

the Inn? Charlotte gave Davis a questioning look. He didn't respond because he was watching Sam with such intensity Charlotte felt her stomach twist into a knot.

Sam's gaze slid to Bella, "And you are?"

"Bella Velez," Bella answered, not a smidge of insecurity in her response.

"Right, the assistant," Sam dropped her eyes to Bill's used dishes in front of her. A silent request, but a request nonetheless.

A cloud passed over Bella's face and she moved to stand up and clear the dishes. Charlotte jumped up faster. She was not going to allow Bella to be humiliated by this woman.

"I'll get it," Davis was right behind Charlotte, stepping quickly to his ex-wife's side and making a neat pile of the used dishes. Sam watched him lift them off the table, a flicker of amusement crossing her impeccable face. He never took his eyes off of her.

Charlotte thought she might be sick. The arrival of Sam at their loveliest of Christmas dinners was bad enough, but Davis' reaction to his ex-wife made her feel like she was spinning on a teetering carnival ride. Where she'd felt sparkly and joyful a few minutes ago, she now felt nauseated and anxious, even guilty.

All of the bright, exciting potential of their new romance was splintering right in front of her eyes. She wasn't the newfound love of his life. The woman he'd loved and married was sitting right there in front of her face, and there was no comparison. Where Charlotte was short and round, Sam was tall and slender. Where Charlotte was average, Sam was exotic. And more than anything else, Charlotte wasn't even the one thing that everyone thought she was, a talented chef. She sat there at a table decorated with kindergarten crafts feeling like a short, fat, unlovable fraud. But what was really hard to swallow was she had become completely invisible to Davis since Sam walked into the room.

Instead of ending with a memorable toast or moment of shared joy, Christmas dinner simply dispersed. Bella prepared a hot chocolate to-go bag for Denny and Vicky to take on their sleigh ride, Bill escaped to the barn to hitch up the horses, Denny and Vicky dressed the Biddlebumps in their down jackets, and Davis disappeared with Sam somewhere inside the Inn.

Charlotte sat at the table, unable to think of a reason to get up. Her head hurt and her face felt like it was stretching down towards the floor, like she'd never be able to smile again.

Everything she and Davis had done together was gone, swept away on a bitter cold wind named Sam, leaving Charlotte alone. The same feeling she used to get as a child when Christmas was over, when all of the presents were opened, and there was nothing more to celebrate, crept through her. It was empty, lonely, and sad.

Her eyes drifted across the table. It was littered with dirty plates and glasses, used napkins in crumpled piles, and candles burned to their stubs, misshapen blobs of wax hanging precariously off their edges. Everything was a mess. A darkness surrounded her and Charlotte tasted hot tears at the back of her throat.

"I'll take this out to them," Bella informed her as she carried the sleigh ride treats out the kitchen door towards the foyer. The Biddlebumps were barking and whining. They were excited to go outside in the snow. Flashes of her romantic sleigh ride flew through her mind. Could that really have been just a few hours ago? It felt like it happened weeks ago, if it had happened at all.

She wondered where Davis was right now. What was he doing with Sam? Were they talking? Arguing? Making up?

That thought was too much to take. Charlotte pushed her chair back and escaped from the kitchen before Bella returned, hoping against hope that she wouldn't run into Davis and Sam on her way up to her room.

After a good cry, Charlotte washed her face with cold water and tried to fix her hair and makeup so she didn't look so puffy and undone. Her attempts didn't really work and soon she gave up. What she wanted to do was stay in her room, put on her pajamas, and crawl into bed. What she needed to do, however, was return to the kitchen and help clean up. Bella must be exhausted.

She didn't expect to see Davis washing dishes, a tea towel tossed over his shoulder, his sleeves rolled up, and his hands in a sink full of bubbles. He looked up at her when she walked in, distracted.

"I...uh, I told Bella to take a chair for a while," he said, his eyes not quite meeting hers.

"Oh..." nothing more came to mind to say to him. Nothing at all.

Charlotte moved stiffly past him to the table, which was still a mess. She began stacking plates and silverware and took them in armloads to the island. She couldn't bring herself to take them all the way to the sink, so close to where he stood. When that was done she turned her attention to pulling down the paper snowflakes and stars.

"Don't take those," Davis interrupted. He had turned to collect the dishes she'd brought to the island, his arms dripping dishwater, "Please." He was looking at her, really looking at her, for the first time since their dinner was destroyed. He looked strained and more than just a little bit guilty.

Charlotte's hand was hanging in mid air where it had frozen when he spoke. She let it drop to her side.

"Thanks," he gave her his usually charming half smile, but there was no light in his eyes. He sighed and looked away from her, placing his hands on the edge of the island as if he was bracing himself. He started speaking without looking up, "I know this is really, really awkward." He lifted his eyes to hers, capturing them and holding them like he always could, "All I want is—"

"What are you doing?"

Sam's voice cut through the room so unexpectedly Charlotte jumped. Davis straightened, though he didn't turn towards her. His face hardened and Charlotte could tell their little moment was over. His wife was back. He was done talking.

"What do you need, Sam?" He asked.

Charlotte wished she could sink into the floor and avoid all of this.

Sam slid into the room, like a swan gliding gracefully across the water. As she walked past Davis she touched the small of his back, letting her fingers slip around his waist. His eyes were on Charlotte as she watched the move, then he dropped his gaze to the floor, the tiny muscles in his jaw flexing. Sam stopped just past him, placing her arms elegantly across her chest in a displeased stance.

"Why are you doing the dishes, darling?"

"Don't," was all he said. He kept his eyes trained on the floor in front of him.

"I'm pretty sure the help can handle cleaning up," her lips made a tiny smacking sound on 'up'. Once again, Charlotte felt the hackles rise on her neck. "Where is the other one?" Sam asked, making a faux attempt to look around the room.

"Her name is Bella," Charlotte said.

"Right, where is Bella?"

"I told her to take a break," Davis grabbed a stack of dishes and turned back to the sink.

"Hang on," Sam raised one finger into the air as if testing the wind direction. "Tell me you haven't been washing dishes the whole time Denny and Vicky have been here," Sam glared at Davis' back. There was something offensive the way she used Denny and Vicky's first names, like she'd known them forever. Charlotte's face flushed with anger, then with shame as Sam's glare turned on her. "We paid you and your assistant a significant amount of money to handle this for us," her irritation was obvious, and justified. Charlotte's stomach felt like stone.

"Leave it alone, Sam," Davis turned from the sink as he spoke, his eyes were sharp.

"I'm not going to leave it alone," she imitated his deep voice on the last part of her sentence, mocking him.

"She missed her flight," Charlotte tried to explain, but her voice came out in almost a whisper. Of course it looked bad, but that's not how it had been, had it? She looked to Davis, hoping he was going to step in and make it better somehow.

"Vicky said something about your famous chili," Sam said with disbelief. "Were you cooking?" She barked a laugh at the realization. Her beautiful mouth hung open like a disgusted teenager as she gawked at Davis.

"It's not your business—" he started, his cheeks turning red with anger or embarrassment, Charlotte wasn't sure.

"Oh, it most definitely is my business," Sam shoved her chin at him as she spat out the words. Her beautiful eyes were narrowed to slits, "The money we spent is my business."

Charlotte couldn't take it anymore. She wanted nothing more than to get out of that kitchen, out of the Inn completely.

"Look," she interrupted. She'd found her voice, finally, "There were some unavoidable problems the first few days and we worked them out. Luckily Dav—Mr. Reed was flexible and supportive. Of course, we will refund the entire fee."

Sam closed her mouth and gave Charlotte a once over. Charlotte knew this type of woman, the perfect abs, the toned everything. She knew when a woman like that was feeling prettier than her, when she was checking off an internal list of everything that was wrong with Charlotte's body. It was the final humiliation of her day when Sam finished her silent judgment and smirked. She'd won. In so many ways Sam had won and Charlotte knew it.

"Now, if you'll excuse me," Charlotte made her way towards the door. She avoided Sam's eyes, but gave Davis a pointed look, "Please let us do the cleaning up, Mr. Reed. Bella and I will take care of everything."

She left the kitchen so fast he didn't have a chance to respond.

CHAPTER 17

Charlotte didn't sleep a wink all night. After enduring Sam's scathing accusations then exiting the kitchen, she found Bella upstairs and told her the whole story with only intermittent moments of bawling.

Bella listened with all of the passion and empathy of a good friend, only partly surprised. She had guessed something was going on between the two of them ever since arriving.

"And you think he was leading you on the whole time?" She asked, after Charlotte explained the way Davis seemed to be letting Sam take over.

Charlotte gave a half-hearted shrug, her face screwing into a crumpled sad mess as she fought back more tears. He had not struck her as a playboy type, but what else was she supposed to think now? Bella clucked her tongue a few times, shaking her head at the way her friend had been misused.

"I heard him showing her to a room," Bella informed her. "So she's staying the night here. I don't think we're going to be rid of her," she watched for Charlotte's reaction, which was a mix of horror and heartbreak. Bella reached out and patted her friend's hand, "I'll tell them you're not feeling well, Charlie. You need to go to bed."

Before Charlotte did what she was told, she insisted on helping Bella clean the kitchen. As soon as that was done, she retreated to her room and cried herself out. When that was done, she was left with a throbbing headache and stuffed up nose, making her toss and turn all night.

She only emerged in the morning out of a guilty sense of duty. If all she was to Davis was the hired help, she wouldn't give him, or Sam, the satisfaction of quitting. Charlotte was a lot of things, but she was not a quitter.

Breakfast turned out to be a dull affair. The food was good, actually the food was fantastic, thanks to Bella. However, the mood that had bonded them all together during the heavy snow and the Christmas activities was broken. Sam didn't come down to breakfast, ordering it delivered to her room instead. Still, her presence was felt and it left a thin film of discomfort on everyone.

Bella, very conscious that Sam was keeping an eye on them and their performance in the kitchen, went above and beyond with breakfast. She also took Sam her tray. Charlotte offered to deliver the meal so her friend didn't have to suffer Sam's particular style of humiliation.

"No, I'm taking it," Bella said, eyeing Charlotte's puffy face and general depressed demeanor. "You're not in a good space," she stated.

"I'm sorry," Charlotte felt miserable that she couldn't stand up to this situation with anything that resembled grace.

Bella gave Charlotte a sympathetic look, "It's okay, Charlie. You've got a bad case of the love bug." She shrugged, "Besides, I'm the one that got us into this. Even if she is horrible, we leave tomorrow and it's all over!"

There was that bit of cheery news, as well. They were leaving tomorrow. They'd been able to cash in their return tickets, which would help in paying back the fee they'd received for this gig in the first place. Charlotte would ride back to Seattle with Bella, a two-day trip that they needed to start early the next day. They were booked to be on Seattle's favorite morning show on New Year's Eve to give tips on how to throw a great party.

Charlotte was torn. She wanted to go home, that was for sure. Being back at her house in her normal routine was so appealing after suffering through the rapid dissolving of her holiday romance. But part of her knew that leaving here would be the last time she ever laid eyes on Davis, and that thought tore at her heart. Being here with him at the Inn had been wonderful, even if only briefly.

After Bella disappeared with Sam's tray the others arrived. Davis looked tired. Charlotte wondered if he had stayed up with Sam. Had they reconciled? Had they slept together? The thought sent a new rush of emotions through her and she focused hard on pouring a cup of coffee. There was no way she would be able to eat.

"It looks like the snow isn't going to last much longer," Denny observed. He stood at the kitchen window and looked out over the yard and distant woods. The relentless mountain sunshine was doing its job on the treetops and fence posts, which held only remnants of ice and snow. Though the larger drifts on the ground remained, the walkways and driveway were clear. The snow couple Davis had built were misshapen blobs now, their stick arms no longer holding on to one another.

Charlotte joined Denny looking out the window. She thought about how the melting of the snow that had bound them all together was symbolic of the fact that their time here was over. Bernie and Blanche snuffled around her feet, begging for attention as if they could tell she was already missing them.

"Good morning, Biddlebumps," she managed a smile as she reached down to scratch their fat little heads.

"It comes then goes," Davis' voice surprised her, he was standing behind her and she tried not to look at him. She didn't trust her reaction. "The snow," he clarified.

She couldn't help but glance back at him, his eyes were plaintive. A jolt of sorrow washed through her and she had to look away.

"Will Sam be joining us?" Vicky asked as she eyed the tomato and goat cheese frittata on the table. Charlotte couldn't be completely sure, but it felt like the older woman was making sure the coast was clear more than she was missing Sam's company.

"No, she's still in her room," Davis answered.

Bill scoffed then quickly covered it up by pretending he was coughing.

"Bella just took up her breakfast," Charlotte added, giving Vicky a clearer idea of how long the newest arrival intended to stay away.

Vicky looked to Denny then to Davis then back again, "Maybe we should talk business over breakfast?"

Her suggestion was so mild, so matter of fact, yet Charlotte could detect meaning in it. She wondered if the men had picked up on what she was doing. Vicky didn't like Sam, Charlotte was sure of it, and she obviously wanted to keep Sam out of their business discussion.

"Now?" Denny sat down at the table with his coffee.

"Well," Vicky picked up Blanche and settled her in her lap. "We leave tomorrow morning and I know you wanted to do some more snowshoeing or something this afternoon, get in some more outdoor time," she took a sip of her coffee while giving Charlotte an almost imperceptible smile.

"That's true," Denny agreed. He looked at Davis who

seemed surprised and hopeful, like a man stuck in a hole who'd just been thrown a rope, "What do you say, Davis?"

"Sure, absolutely," he answered. "I could bring the paperwork in here..."

"Oh, no," Vicky waved that suggestion away. "Let's go to your office. It will be more convenient," she waited for Denny to agree, which he did immediately.

Davis was flustered. He was looking over the delicious breakfast Bella had put out for them and feeling bad about pulling his guests away from it.

"Why don't I fix you a tray and bring it to the office?" Charlotte blurted out without thinking.

Vicky grinned at her, "That would be lovely, Charlotte."

Davis was frozen, the conversation so quickly turning to what might be his favor seemed to have put him in shock. He looked at her and she could tell he didn't know what to say. In that moment she took pity on him. All of the things he'd shared with her about growing up here and his worries over impressing Denny and Vicky so he could save the Inn from foreclosure came to the forefront. She gave him an encouraging smile.

"Go on, I'll bring it in to you in a few minutes," she said.

"Thank you," he gushed. There was no doubt in her mind that he meant it.

Charlotte put together two beautiful trays containing generous pieces of the frittata, fresh scones, and sliced fruit within minutes. She provided small plates, silverware and a thermal carafe of coffee with all of the fixings as well. There was a strong sense that they needed to stay in the office without interruption for as long as possible.

"Let me help you," Bill offered as she lifted the first tray. He took up the second one and followed her down the hallway.

They dropped the trays off and stepped out of the office

as unobtrusively as possible. Charlotte pulled the door shut and shared a look with Bill.

"Now we keep our fingers crossed," he whispered.

The excitement of Denny and Vicky possibly investing in the Inn infiltrated her sorrowful mood. Maybe everything wasn't a total loss. At least she had done something nice in helping Davis keep this beautiful place in his family. Her mood lifted a little as she joined Bella in cleaning up breakfast and planning for their last day.

Bill finished his breakfast at the kitchen table and engaged them in conversation. He told them stories about his childhood growing up in the mountains, cougar sightings, the time he'd taken Davis as a little boy on a horseback ride and a massive bull elk had run out in front of them causing the horse to buck so hard Bill had fallen off, but not Davis.

"That little kid hung on for dear life," Bill chuckled at the memory. "He had hold of that saddle horn and he was not letting go. He's never been one to give up," he added.

Just then a yawning Sam wandered into the kitchen.

"Even when he should cut bait and run," Bill added just loud enough for Charlotte and Bella to hear.

Though not completely awake, Sam still looked like a model in her sexy-slouchy lounge pants and a loose knit grey sweater that fell nicely over her curves. It was amazing what great clothes and perfect good looks did for a person.

"Where's Davis?" She asked, skipping over any morning greetings.

Charlotte and Bella looked at each other then at Bill, who was carefully sipping his coffee. He didn't answer so they didn't either.

"Bill?" Sam's annoyance was obvious.

"Good morning," he said as if he'd just seen her walk in the room.

She rolled her eyes, "Where's Davis?"

He looked out the window like he was searching for him outside in the snow, "Not sure."

She sighed heavily and turned her attention to Charlotte and Bella, "Is there coffee?"

"Yes," Bella stood and indicated with a quick shake of her head at Charlotte that she would take care of Sam's demands.

"I need to talk to him," Sam complained as she flopped into the chair Bella had just vacated.

"I was thinking," Bill ignored Sam and spoke directly to Charlotte, "you ladies never got a tour of the barn and outbuildings because of the snow. Since the weather's warmed up, would you like to take that tour now?"

They jumped on the chance to get out of the kitchen and away from Sam. Charlotte worried a little that Sam might go looking for Davis in the office, but there wasn't a lot they could do about that. He'd been alone with Denny and Vicky for over an hour now, hopefully that was enough privacy.

Outside the day was brilliant, it almost felt balmy compared to the previous cold, especially when they walked through the sunshine. Charlotte didn't zip up her jacket or put on her hat and gloves. Neither did Bella.

"Thank you, Bill," Charlotte told him when they were out of earshot of the house.

"Yes, thank you for getting us out of the kitchen. Our presence seems to annoy her," Bella added.

"Who, Sam?" Bill asked. They nodded in response and Bill chuckled, shaking his head. "Sam is always annoyed. She likes causing problems, stirring the pot, you know?" Again, they nodded. "I thought we'd seen the last of her when those two broke up at the beginning of the year, but I suppose there's still a few loose ends."

They were at the barn now and Bill swung the huge doors open, letting in the crisp, sunny day. He showed Bella the workbench where Charlotte had helped Denny make Vicky's

Christmas wreath. He led them through another door into a large tack room and out the back end of that room into a long corridor. The horses were kept in stalls there and Charlotte and Bella cooed over them to their heart's content.

The beautiful bays were both mares, tall and stately, with velvety soft noses that blew warm air on Charlotte's palm when she held it out to them. Bill gave them slices of apples to feed the horses while he opened the doors on the outside of their stalls so they were free to enjoy the day in their paddock.

"This one's Daisy," Bill told Charlotte as he stroked the white spot on the horse's forehead.

"Hello, Daisy," Charlotte smiled and fed her another apple slice.

"And this one?" Bella asked, obviously charmed by the mare she was petting.

"That's Peanut."

Both girls giggled.

"Well, nice to meet you, Peanut," Bella said.

They spent quite a while outside with Bill, helping him feed Daisy and Peanut their oats and hay for the morning. Being out in the fresh air around those beautiful animals got her mind off of her own problems. After a while Charlotte noticed that the change of scenery had really lifted her mood. She was feeling quite a bit better and enjoyed petting the shining hair on the horses strong necks and their lush, sensitive noses. Just as she was beginning to wonder if they should go back to the Inn and start fixing lunch she heard the door to the tack room open and shut.

Charlotte's stomach did a little flip flop. Daisy and Peanut's ears perked up and they stuck their heads out of their stalls. Daisy whinnied in anticipation and moments later Davis walked out of the tack room, stopping short when his eyes locked on Charlotte's.

He hadn't expected to see her there.

Charlotte glanced over to where she thought Bella was standing at the back of the barn. She was gone. The sound of Bella's voice talking to Bill floated to them from somewhere out in the paddock. She looked back at Davis, her eyes wide. He hadn't moved. Her heart started beating rapidly and her hands began to sweat.

Dust particles floated through the sunrays that shone through the open doors. Davis wore jeans and a red flannel shirt. He looked tired and unshaven, and sexy, with his dark hair in disarray. The horses stamped impatiently in their stalls, excited at seeing Davis or perhaps sensing the emotional tension rising between them. Charlotte didn't know. She couldn't speak. Her heart was in her throat.

They were alone and time had stopped.

CHAPTER 18

"You're here," Davis said. The sound of his voice sent a tingle over her skin. Not good. She needed to keep her head and make sound judgments, all while in the dim, rustic beauty of this old barn in the mountains with this man, the man she might have fallen in love with.

"I'm here," she managed to answer.

Daisy whinnied again, backing up Charlotte's statement. Comedic relief.

Davis seemed to relax, as if he'd been holding his breath and didn't have to anymore. His mouth pulled up on one side and he half smiled, a tiny twinkle in his eyes.

"I see you've met Daisy," he walked towards her. With every step he took, a small chill rippled along Charlotte's backbone. He stopped on the other side of the horse, who affectionately nudged his chest. "Hi, girl," he pulled a sugar cube out of his pocket and offered it to Daisy, who gobbled it greedily. "I was looking for you," he said, his voice low.

Charlotte wrinkled her brow. Was he talking to her or the horse?

"Me?"

"Yes, you."

She blushed at the misunderstanding, and at his words. She turned her face towards Daisy, pretending to look intently at her mane.

"I wanted to talk to you," he said, watching her evenly.

"Oh?" She kept her focus on the horse's mane and tried to appear calm, "About what?"

"About everything."

She looked at him then, giving him her best nonchalant What Could Possibly Be Wrong face, "Everything?"

He stepped around Daisy's head so they were on the same side of the horse and Charlotte couldn't avoid eye contact, "You know what I mean. Sam. I didn't know she was coming and since she's been here it's been..." He searched for a word and found it, "Weird."

Charlotte scoffed so hard it came out as a snort, causing Daisy to rear her head back in surprise.

"Is it that bad?" His face was sheepish.

"Of course it's weird," Charlotte said. "She's your ex-wife!" The heat in her cheeks grew hotter.

He furrowed his brow, considering her embarrassment before he spoke, "You and I haven't done anything wrong."

The memory of cuddling with him on the couch, the way he kissed her so sweetly under the mistletoe and on the sleigh ride filled her mind, making her cheeks burn.

"I don't fool around with married men," Charlotte tried to explain.

"I'm not married. Not anymore."

"Tell that to Sam," she said, sharper than she intended.

Davis was taken aback for a second at her reaction.

"What exactly do you think is going on with Sam and I?" He asked, searching her eyes for an answer.

Charlotte couldn't look away from him, but she felt anger

flash across her already flushed face as she answered, "It's pretty obvious."

"Not to me."

All of the hurt and insecurity she'd felt since meeting Sam rose to the surface. Hot tears filled her eyes and her chin trembled as she spoke, "She's so beautiful."

Davis raised his eyebrows in surprise. He reached out and took her hand in his, "You're beautiful."

Charlotte shook her head, tears now rolled down her cheeks and she was helpless to stop them.

"She's your wife," she argued.

"She was my wife, but she's not anymore," he squeezed her hands. "And I'm not interested in going back, believe me."

Charlotte shook his comment off, "I know she's your ex-wife, but she has some kind of hold on you." She gave him a reproachful look, "And she's not just beautiful, she's drop dead gorgeous."

Davis laughed, his eyes shining as he pulled her closer to him, "She doesn't have any kind of hold on me. And looks aren't everything, you know."

She let him wrap his arms around her in a hug. She wanted to lose herself in his arms, breathe him in while he held her close, but there were bigger problems to deal with, and he wasn't being honest with her or himself. Sam did have some kind of hold on him, whether he admitted it or not. Charlotte pushed gently away from him.

"You've been very different since she got here," she said.

He started to laugh off her comment, but stopped when he saw the look on her face. He dropped his gaze to his feet and sighed, then threw his head back and growled at the wooden rafters in the barn. When he looked at her again, his eyes were pained, worried, sad.

"You're right, I guess. She does have one last vice grip on

me," he let his gaze move around the room, landed on Daisy in her stall, then came back to Charlotte. "This place. She knows I need Denny and Vicky to make it work and I think...I think she came here to mess with that...to mess with me."

"To sabotage their visit?"

He nodded, "Yes, I think so." He took her by the arms gently, buckling his knees a little so he was looking her straight in the eye, "But it's nothing more than that. I promise you. I need to keep her under control until everything with Denny and Vicky is done. As soon as their lawyer reviews the contract we went over this morning, they'll sign it, I'll sign it and there will be nothing she can do to me anymore."

Charlotte was glad for him, truly. She knew what the Inn meant to him. He must be under so much stress trying to keep it running with someone like Sam lurking in the background hoping he failed, actively trying to make him fail. She wondered what their marriage had been like. What kind of wife had she been? What had he suffered trying to make her happy?

"Davis?" The voice was unmistakable, impatiently annoyed.

Davis stiffened. The light in his eyes hardened, going from gentle humor to anger in a split second. He straightened and turned towards the tack room door where Sam stood glaring at them. Davis stepped sideways so his body partially blocked Charlotte from his ex-wife. An instinctive move of protection.

"What do you want, Sam?"

To Charlotte, his body language was obvious, screaming at Sam to go away. Sam, however, ignored his body language and did the exact opposite. She slid her eyes to Charlotte halfway hidden behind Davis then focused on him and him alone. She lowered her lashes seductively as she walked slowly towards him, a sultry smirk on her full mouth.

"What do you want?" He asked again. His back was rigid, his hands clenched at his sides.

"I've been looking for you," her tone was higher than normal, girlish.

"You found me, what do you need?" Charlotte heard the controlled irritation in his voice. Either Sam was oblivious to social cues or she liked getting under his skin. It was almost certainly the latter.

Again, Sam's beautiful green-blue eyes shot a look at Charlotte. It was all she could do to not lean over and hide completely behind Davis' broad back.

"Not in front of the help," Sam said.

Though she couldn't see his face, Charlotte heard the frustrated fury in his voice, "That's enough."

Charlotte stepped out from behind him, "It's all right." She put her hand on Davis' arm to calm him, "I need to get back, it's almost time for lunch."

"Charlotte you don't–" he started.

"Thank you, Chef Charlotte, you're very thoughtful," Sam interrupted.

"No problem," Charlotte said as brightly as she could. She didn't want Sam to know that she got to her. She nodded a quick goodbye to them and left.

Out in the open, Charlotte walked across the muddy driveway towards the Inn and took in a deep breath. The sunny day had lost some of its earlier shine, as had her mood. The thrill of being with Davis alone again, feeling him close, knowing he cared, all of that dissipated when Sam arrived. Maybe everything he said was true and once this deal was done he could wash his hands of her forever, but Sam would always be his first wife. Charlotte wondered if she could honestly handle that if their relationship were to move to the next level.

"Wait up," Bella called out. Charlotte turned to see her friend hurrying from the paddock where she'd just left Bill. As soon as she was close enough for Charlotte to hear her whisper, Bella asked, "What happened in there?"

"What do you mean?"

"Are they arguing?"

Charlotte glanced back at the barn, "Not when I left."

"Well, they are now," Bella fell into step with her then shuddered like she'd just felt a chill. "I don't know how he stands that woman," she added.

"Yeah," Charlotte muttered.

"Bill doesn't like her at all," Bella confessed. Charlotte didn't answer. "He told me that she's been chasing Davis since they were teenagers. Always hanging around, pushing her way into the family, strutting her stuff, using her looks to get him to notice her, and he eventually caved in to the temptation. Then she told him she was pregnant to get him to marry her!"

"She did?" Charlotte felt a twinge of sympathy for a young, sweet Davis stuck in the web of that manipulative woman, "Was she?"

Bella scoffed, "Of course not." She waved her hand backwards at the barn, "Women like that never tell the truth about such things. They're, what's the word?" Bella searched her internal Spanish to English dictionary, "Malcriada...so bratty."

"Yeah, I guess so," Charlotte felt the sympathy for Davis turn into sadness for the whole situation.

Bella looked at her friend, shaking her head and making 'tsk-tsk' sounds, "But you like him a lot, don't you?"

Charlotte nodded.

"You don't want to leave tomorrow?"

"Yes and no."

"What yes and what no?"

Charlotte sighed, they had reached the Inn now and stood at the fence that led to the red front door.

"I want to leave because I just want to go home and get back to normal, you know? Also, we have that thing on New Year's Eve."

Bella dismissed their New Year's Eve commitment with a wrinkle of her nose, but nodded her understanding and waited for Charlotte to finish.

"But..." Charlotte's lip quivered slightly as she spoke, "I'm so sad at the idea of leaving here, of leaving him." She dropped her eyes to the ground.

"Oh, Charlie," Bella pulled her into a hug. "I'm so sorry, my friend," she squeezed Charlotte tightly, then held her out at arm's length, "Love is a terrible, horrible, terrible thing."

Charlotte had to laugh at Bella's drama. She wiped the tears from her cheeks and let out a frustrated sigh, "Yes, it is."

"We will do whatever you want. We can stay a little longer or we will drive away tomorrow morning and get back to life. It's up to you," Bella told her, resolute in her determination to be supportive no matter what.

Charlotte remained unsure what to do. The rest of the day was spent mostly with Bella in the kitchen or tactfully avoiding interactions with Sam. Every time Davis entered a room on his own, Sam was close on his heels. He was like a haunted man, stress stretched over his face, and Charlotte empathized with his strain. She hoped the contract would be returned soon and get signed and everything would be over, but she was worried that it wouldn't really be over, not ever.

Right before dinner she went to her room to pack. If they were going to leave tomorrow she wanted to be ready. It would be hard enough to drive away from this place, she didn't want to have the extra panic of last minute packing weighing on her mind.

A soft knock on her door did not make her curious. She was expecting Bella to pop in any time.

"Come in," she said.

The door swung open and, much to her surprise, Charlotte saw Bill standing awkwardly in the hallway.

"Bill?"

"I don't mean to bother you," he said.

"It's fine," she said as she walked to the door and ushered him in, closing the door behind them. "What can I do for you?"

"I wondered if I couldn't talk to you for a few minutes," Bill said.

"Sure," Charlotte smiled at him. He was rough and worn on the outside, decades of hard work and mountain living, but she believed he was one of the kindest men she'd ever met. He looked charmingly uncomfortable standing in her hotel room with his hat in his hands.

"I know this may be none of my business," he started, his cheeks reddening just a little.

"Go ahead, Bill, tell me what's on your mind," she encouraged.

"Well, I've noticed that you and Davis seem to have taken a real shine to each other," Bill began. It was Charlotte's turn to blush. Was their romance that obvious to everyone? "Now, don't feel shy about it," Bill reassured her. "It's a good thing to see two nice young people carrying on with each other, a happy thing."

Charlotte sat down on the edge of her bed, more than a little embarrassed about what Bill may have to say.

"I didn't realize we were being so obvious," she said.

"It may not be to everyone, but I've known Davis since he

was born. There's not a lot that goes on with that boy that doesn't show itself to me somehow."

Charlotte was slightly relieved, but only slightly.

"I came up here to tell you...well, to let you know that..." he was having a hard time getting the words out.

"What do you think I should know?" Charlotte asked.

Bill peered at her from underneath his bushy, white eyebrows, "I've never seen him as happy as he is when he's with you."

Charlotte's heart skipped a beat.

"He lights up when you're in the room, and the way you two got along putting on Christmas here at the Inn...well, it reminded me a lot of his Mom and Dad," he gave her a wistful smile. "Now, I know Sam showing up hasn't been a bed of roses," he spoke her name like it tasted bad in his mouth. "She's always been a bad egg and Davis finally got himself out of that mess," he shook his head slowly. "For her to show up again like this is just plain old spite," he paused.

"Bill, I appreciate what you're saying, it's very sweet."

Bill held up his hand to stop her talking, "I don't mean to stick my nose into your business or anything. I just wanted to tell you something that I think is important."

"Okay," she said, waiting.

"Davis Reed is one of the finest men you'll ever know. He's going through a rough patch at the moment, but if you were to decide on him, you wouldn't be sorry. Not ever."

Sweet, old Bill. Charlotte was overcome at his devotion to Davis and his attempt to help their floundering romance along. She thanked him for his thoughts and he made his apologies again for interfering before shuffling out the door.

Charlotte was left alone with her half packed bag and conflicting emotions.

On one hand, there were so many things about Davis and this place that were right, plain and simple. She couldn't deny the intense feelings she had for him and the joy they'd had together over Christmas. On the other hand, the turmoil of his life at the moment, Sam's arrival, and Charlotte's life that waited in Seattle, were all reasons to question if a romance was the best idea right now.

Bill's plea for Davis had been heartwarming. Charlotte knew he meant it and that he was probably right, Davis was a good guy. But the plea hadn't come directly from Davis, and she could not ignore that fact.

Charlotte sighed heavily and let her eyes wander over the beautiful room. Thoughts of Davis ran through her mind; the sound of his laugh, the feel of him gently touching her face right before they kissed, the way he looked when he was strumming the guitar, or cooking at the stove, or playing with the Biddlebumps. Her eyes fell on her half packed suitcase and she felt a pang of grief as she realized the choice she must make.

Her time was up. The magic of Christmas was over. It was possible she might be in love with Davis Reed, but their romance was not going to work itself out in less than twelve hours. She owed it to Bella to get back to their cooking show, and she owed it to herself to return to her life with wonderful memories of this Christmas and her heart intact.

CHAPTER 19

They saw Denny and Vicky and the Biddlebumps off at seven the next morning. Denny had ordered a car to pick them up and he and Vicky were happily involved in settling Bernie and Blanche into the back seat of an extra long SUV just as the sun came up.

Bella pushed a bag of fresh orange cranberry muffins into Denny's hands as they said their goodbyes.

"Thank you, Bella," Denny said warmly, giving her shoulders a firm hug.

"Thank you for everything, Charlotte," Vicky said. "It was delightful to meet you in person, both of you," she kissed Charlotte and Bella both on the cheek.

"And you two," Denny threw one arm around Bill and one around Davis, which was a stretch because they were both so much taller than the friendly dentist. "We'll be seeing both of you in a few months!"

The deal had been sealed, so to speak, early this morning. The Foss' lawyer had emailed the approved contract around five in the morning. Davis printed the contract and had them ready to be signed when everyone woke up. Relief was apparent on his face as he shook Denny's hand.

"I'm looking forward to it," Davis said whole-heartedly.

"And maybe you, too?" Vicky asked Charlotte quietly, a conspiratorial look in her eye.

Charlotte dropped her gaze. The comment made her sad, but she didn't want Vicky to know her innocent jest had caused her any pain. She was not that shocked at Vicky's insinuation after Bill had let her know that the flirty, fun times she'd had with Davis were, in fact, noticed by everyone at the Inn. Still, since things weren't working out, she didn't want Vicky to feel bad about bringing it up.

"I guess we'll see," she answered, giving as generic an answer as possible.

Soon their driver had loaded all of their luggage and Bill, Bella, Charlotte and Davis waved to the SUV as it rolled down the driveway. Sam hadn't gotten out of bed, yet.

Davis turned to them, excitement dancing in his eyes. He made two fists, shook them in the air and exclaimed, "We did it!"

He grabbed Charlotte around the waist and gave her a little twirl. Then he remembered himself and stopped, leaving her breathless. There was an extra long pause and Charlotte knew if nobody else had been there, he would have kissed her. But they were there and he didn't. He let go of her, slightly abashed, then turned to Bill and slapped him on the back.

"We did it, Bill!"

"Good, good for you," Bill answered, his eyes shining with pride.

"Congratulations," Bella said kindly.

Davis rocked back and forth on his heels, full of energy, "Is anyone else starving?"

Bella chimed in, "There are muffins in the kitchen and a quiche in the fridge."

"And fresh coffee," Charlotte reminded her.

"Yes, there's coffee ready," Bella added. "But we are hitting the road," she looked to Charlotte who nodded in agreement.

"You're leaving...now?" Davis asked, surprised.

"Yes," Charlotte was confused at his response. She'd told him at dinner the night before and he hadn't seemed affected. Why was he so shocked?

"Today?" He verified.

"Yes, today," she answered, "I told you last night."

"You did?"

He was undone. His short-lived elation washed away as the reality of their departure sunk in. Charlotte was stunned at his reaction. Could he really have been that distracted that he didn't hear her tell him she was leaving today?

"Our bags are in the foyer," Charlotte told him, trying to explain that this was not a last minute decision. They had actually planned on it.

Davis stared at her, his mind clicking through his memories of the last few days and coming up short.

"I don't...there's...you're going back to Seattle right now?" He pointed at the ground with both of his fore fingers as if they were standing on a giant clock.

"Yes," she said firmly, though she could feel her resolve weakening.

His shoulders slumped and he watched helplessly as Bill went to retrieve their bags and Bella went to pull her car up to the door. Davis raked his hand through his hair, making it stand up almost on end and lending to his bewildered demeanor. Charlotte felt the need to explain.

"We have to be on Today in Seattle on New Year's Eve. I need to go back to work," the excuse fell a little flat, she knew, given that he was one of the only people alive who was aware Chef Charlotte couldn't actually cook.

"Right, of course," he said. He stood in front of her, his eyes brimming with dashed hopes. "I'm sorry, Charlotte. I'm sorry I've been so distracted. This whole thing has been such a mess," he gestured towards the Inn and the surrounding area. Then he reached out and took her by the shoulders, looking deeply into her eyes, "You weren't a mess. Everything we did, everything you helped me with...it was the best." He gave her a sorrowful smile and it poked at her heart, "You're the best, Charlotte."

She started to answer, but Davis leaned down and kissed her full on the mouth before she could say anything. He slid his hands from her shoulders to her neck and up until he was holding her face, kissing her like he never wanted to stop.

Bella's car started in the near distance and Davis pulled away, dropping his hands and shoving them into his pockets. Charlotte stayed lost in his kiss for a few moments longer, unable to speak, the feel of his hands and lips still warm on her skin.

Bill came out the front door carrying luggage and Bella pulled the car up next to him so they could load the trunk. Charlotte wasn't much help. She felt like she'd been turned into marble, a statue doomed to watch the movements of the world around her and stare unmoving at the man she loved, forever. Never allowed to touch him or kiss him again. Her heart twisted and she had to concentrate on breathing.

"That's everything," Bill announced as he slammed the trunk shut.

"Ready, Charlie?" Bella asked, looking from Charlotte to Davis and back again.

Charlotte nodded and Bill stepped in front of her to give her a quick hug. Bella hugged Davis. Then they switched. As Bill hugged Bella, Davis took Charlotte quickly in his arms, squeezing her for only a moment before pushing away, as if he was afraid he wouldn't be able to let her go if he held for more than an instant.

And then she was in the car, driving away from the Inn and back to her real life, Davis Reed quickly becoming part of her past.

CHAPTER 20

I n order to be ready for their 8:22 am spot on Today in Seattle, Charlotte and Bella had a 5:00 am call time. They had an hour in hair and makeup, then were sent to the dresser, then finally had a little over an hour to ready their presentation. For this holiday show Bella had decided on Cajun crab puffs, strawberry margarita cheesecake bites, and a rosemary and thyme champagne cocktail that turned a lovely purple color when mixed properly.

Charlotte had insisted on bringing Bella more to the fore-front of this show, because she and her long time partner in crime had devised a plan on their two-day road trip back to Seattle. After much conversation they had come to the conclusion that Charlotte was tired of lying to the world and Bella was tired of being the chef behind the curtain. So, they'd made a new pact.

Charlotte would insist to the producers that Bella become more of a part of the show, presenting recipes and being more involved. They would become equal partners in a team instead of Chef Charlotte and her assistant, building Bella's reputation to the audience. Then, when their contract was up in six months, Charlotte would back out and push the idea of Chef Bella creating a new cooking show of her own.

Today, New Year's Eve, was the first shoot where they were rolling out their plan and, so far, it was going quite well. The morning talent on the feel good show were happy to have Bella involved. She was beautiful and fun and had that extra exotic element with her Spanish accent. Charlotte was grateful to have her take the lead in as many ways as possible, not only because Charlotte was saved the stress of having to pretend to be knowledgeable, but also because her heart just wasn't in it.

The misery she'd endured since leaving Davis and driving home from Colorado was like nothing she'd ever experienced. A darkness hung over her all the time, she cried herself to sleep every night, and moved like a zombie through the day. Bella was the only one who knew what was happening and was, therefore, the only person Charlotte could talk to about her broken heart.

"This will pass, right?" Charlotte asked the night they stayed over in a hotel on the drive home. Charlotte was flat on her back on the bed, staring at the ceiling, fat tears rolling continually down her cheeks.

"Oh, yes, eventually, one way or another," Bella responded.

Charlotte felt like the only way she would ever feel better was to feel nothing at all. She numbed her sorrow with a bottle of wine every night after she returned home. This helped a little, though she woke up puffy with swollen, red eyes and she knew the producers were concerned about their next shooting schedule. She couldn't find the energy to care what they thought. She didn't care about anything at all.

Bella showed up at her house the night before their Today in Seattle spot. She didn't bring wine, because she knew Charlotte was already partaking a bit too much in that department. What she did bring were facials, moisturizers, massage oils, pedicure supplies and some really funny chick flicks.

"You want to look beautiful on TV tomorrow, yes?" Bella asked as she applied a bright blue facemask to Charlotte's cheeks.

"I guess."

"That's not the best answer, but I will take it!"

On the set of Today in Seattle, Charlotte was thankful for Bella's special spa treatment the night before. After hair and makeup were done she looked as good as could be expected given her current mood. She was also glad Bella had distracted her from drinking any wine. Live television had a lot more room for error than when they were filming her little cooking show in the studio that would be edited together and shown at a later date. At least this way her head was clear and she wouldn't make any stupid mistakes.

Today in Seattle had a live studio audience of 300 people. There was a studio kitchen set up on one side of the set where they would give their cooking demonstration along with the show's hosts. A crew of kitchen staff pre-prepared over 300 of both hors d'oeuvres and the champagne cocktail, which were waiting to be passed out to the studio audience as soon as their presentation was complete.

Everything was set. Charlotte was ready. They'd dressed her in a pair of black slacks, a shimmering silver low cut blouse that looked like it was liquid the way it fell in luscious swoops from her shoulders down to her hips. Her dark hair was pulled up into an attractive loose bun and the hair stylist had expertly pulled certain strands out, twirling them tightly, letting them fall in twisting little loops and pinning the ends back into the bun with tiny glittering bobby pins. Lest anyone forget she was there to cook, Charlotte wore a special made black chef's apron with the words

'Chef Charlotte's Christmas' spelled out in red sequins across the front.

Bella, equally done up and donning her own black apron with the same words shining across the front, stood next to Charlotte. They waited quietly for their cue to come out on stage and greet the hosts right before they cut to a commercial break.

From where they stood they could peer into the audience and see some of the people watching from their seats. Bella was doing just that, while Charlotte did breathing exercises and silently listed the names of the crab puff ingredients Bella had given her the night before on a cheat sheet.

"Is that...?" Bella said under her breath.

Charlotte looked up and squinted in the direction Bella was staring, "What?"

"Nothing," Bella said quickly, switching her gaze to the stage in front of them. "Nothing at all."

The demonstration went off without a hitch. Charlotte remembered the names of the ingredients and she directed at least half of the host's questions to Bella to answer as a way to verify her expertise and, hopefully, over time, get Chef Bella some much deserved attention. At the end, Audrey, the female part of the hosting team, asked Charlotte if she wouldn't mind taking some questions from the audience. Charlotte agreed, hoping they weren't going to ask her anything too difficult.

The first question came from an older woman somewhere in the upper right hand side of the crowd. In all truth, Charlotte was partially blinded by the studio lights that shone down on her from the back of the room, so she couldn't see the little lady. She heard the question just fine. The lady wanted to know if Charlotte got to eat in nice restaurants for free now that she was a famous chef.

"Only if I help them wash the dishes," Charlotte quipped. Everyone laughed.

The second question was for Bella. A young woman in the front center wanted to know where she was from and if she, too, wanted to have a cooking show. Perfect question! Charlotte handed the microphone to Bella for her to answer, and smiled and clapped when she was done.

"Time for one more question," Audrey said, pointing somewhere in the upper left section. Charlotte took the microphone back from Bella and tried to see the person who stood up, but again, the lights were too much. It wasn't until she heard his voice that her stomach dropped.

"This question is for Charlotte...Chef Charlotte," the man began. Charlotte knew his voice instantly. Her eyes widened and she snapped them to Bella, who was grinning ear to ear.

"My question is...do you have a recipe for award winning chili?"

Davis. It was Davis. He was here.

Charlotte walked towards the audience, shielding her eyes from the light with her hand, trying to see him in the audience. She realized that everyone was waiting for her to respond.

"Award winning chili?" She asked into the microphone.

"Yes," he answered.

"No, I'm sorry, I don't," she said. She was at the foot of the stairs that led to his section. The lights were no longer glaring into her eyes and she could see him standing at the end of the row, microphone in hand.

"Because if you need a recipe for award winning chili, I have one you can borrow," he said as he walked down the stairs and she walked up, towards him. They met somewhere in the middle and Charlotte didn't know what happened with the microphones or the rest of the studio audience or the hosts of Today in Seattle, because Davis swept her up in his arms and was kissing her on live TV. The crowd started clapping and they cut to commercial break.

"What are you doing here?" Charlotte asked him, the joy in her heart spilled out as laughter.

"I've come for you," Davis told her. "Or to you, whichever you want!"

"What are you talking about?"

"I'm saying what I didn't have time to say before you left," he took both of her hands in his and held them to his heart. "I love you, Charlotte, and I want to be with you," he lifted her hands to his lips and kissed them. "I'm sorry I didn't have it together enough to tell you before you left."

Charlotte felt light headed. This tall, dark, and handsome man was standing in front of hundreds of people declaring his love for her. She thought she might faint.

"At first I thought you should stay with me at the Inn, but then I realized after you left that the Inn without you isn't as wonderful as it is with you. So, if you want to stay in Seattle, I will come to you. You choose."

"Davis," she said, her hands trembled with emotion and he kissed them again.

"That is," he paused, giving her a serious look, "If you love me."

She paused for breath. She couldn't speak, she was so overcome.

"Say it!" A voice shouted out of the audience, another one followed. Charlotte laughed, though she was shaking all over now. Davis held her steadily, waiting patiently for her answer.

"Tell him, Charlie! This is your chance!" Bella's voice rang up from the stage. Comedic relief, again.

"Do you love me, Charlotte?" Davis asked more quietly, his vulnerability showing through. His eyes adoring her and hoping for a 'yes' answer.

She nodded as tears streamed down her cheeks, completely ruining her professional makeup, "I do love you."

The crowd cheered.

Later, when the taping was over, they walked arm and arm through the backstage of Today in Seattle. Crew and staff congratulated them heartily as they passed. Charlotte smiled demurely as Davis thanked them for their good wishes. He stopped at the office of the assistant director, Harvey, and knocked on the door.

Charlotte gave him a questioning look, he just winked at her. The door opened and Harvey ushered them in, then excused himself so they could have some privacy.

"What is this about?" She asked, wondering what he was up to now.

Davis leaned against a long table that spanned one side of the office and cocked his head at her, "Remember how I said I would get you a Christmas gift next year?"

"Yes, I remember," she smiled.

"Well, since tomorrow is technically next year, I thought I would get you a belated gift for this past Christmas and one for tomorrow. So you actually get two gifts."

"How sweet, what did you get for me?"

Davis stood and pulled a large cardboard box with air holes punched into it from underneath the table, "I think, actually, the question should be 'who' did I get you?"

A sharp yipping noise came from the box and Charlotte rushed to its side. When she looked inside she saw a pile of soft blankets and not one, but two puppies staring up at her. They were both all black. One was a soft, fuzzy Lab puppy and one was a tiny, fat, bug eyed Pug.

"Oh, Davis!" She almost squealed with excitement as he leaned down and scooped one into each hand, holding them up next to his face so they were looking at her, but trying to lick his cheeks at the same time.

"It's your own Biddlebump!" He said, laughing.

"You're crazy! And wonderful!" She exclaimed.

"I figured if you rejected me, you wouldn't be able to resist these two."

"I love you all," Charlotte said as she gently took the tiny pug from Davis and gave the lab a kiss on its sweet little nose. "I love you all," she said again.

He smiled at her, his special smile that reached all the way into his eyes and warmed her very soul. Davis made her feel safe and loved and home, and she did love him, just as she knew now for sure that he loved her too. Charlotte tingled with the incredible sense of being alive and present in this moment, connected to this marvelous man. In the deepest part of her heart she understood that this was real and this was forever.

The End

EPILOGUE

Their Christmas tree was a little crooked this year. It had suffered two takedowns by Bacardi, their Lab. They were pretty sure Bacardi had been heavily influenced by the little Pug, Bean. Bacardi and Bean were full grown on the outside, but just being one year old each, were still puppies on the inside. They worked together creating mischief at Crystal Lake Inn, which made life here exciting and hilarious most days.

Today, however, Charlotte was determined to keep the dogs away from the tree long enough that they could finish decorating it and have everything ready for Denny and Vicky, their friends, the Andersons, and the Biddlebumps, of course. They all arrived tomorrow for a Christmas getaway. The Andersons were a human couple, Davis had made sure to double-check this time.

"Honey," Charlotte called to Davis from the kitchen where she was preparing a special mix of dog food, raw eggs and saltine crackers for Bacardi and Bean. She had found that if they were especially full they tended not to get into too much trouble, especially Bean. Bean got very sleepy when he had a full stomach.

"Yeah?" Davis answered. He came to the kitchen from his office where he'd been going over the books for the accountant. It had been a good year here at the Inn. Denny and Vicky's initial investment helped make some improvements and add great new activities for guests. Of course, Bella blurting out the name Crystal Lake Inn when she was being interviewed on Good Morning America about her new cooking show and the antics of Chef Charlotte on New Year's Eve morning TV did wonders for their marketing.

Davis had given Charlotte the choice of where they should live and she had chosen the Inn in the end. It and its owner had charmed her from the very first time she set foot here, and it fast became her home. Everything had all worked out the way Davis told her it would. As soon as he had secured investors he was able to buy Sam out of her portion of the business and send her on her way. They hadn't heard anything from her since.

Charlotte spent every break and holiday from January through May at the Inn with Davis and their pups. She did not renew her contract for the cooking show, just like she and Bella had planned, and was able to move here permanently when it expired in June. Since then she'd been happily helping guests plan for weddings, birthdays and anniversaries at the Inn, as well as decorating for the holidays and managing the staff, which included an amazing chef named Lindsey.

Charlotte paused in her mixing of the dog food treat, much to the chagrin of Bacardi and Bean who were sitting quietly behind her, having heard the can opener and come running. She loved looking at Davis when he first walked into a room. He had an ease about him, a kind of casual sexiness that she didn't think she could ever get tired of observing.

"What do you need, Babe?" He asked.

"I'm going to feed these two so they'll quiet down, then will you have time to help me put up the rest of the decorations?"

He came to her, "Of course." He leaned down and kissed her on the cheek, "I'll even get them fed and let you know when they're mellow so we can get started."

"Perfect," she said. He was the most helpful guy, so willing to do the tedious work. They hadn't talked a lot about kids yet, but Charlotte knew without a doubt that Davis would be a great father when the time came.

Davis took the dog food and whistled so the boys would follow him, "Come on you flea bit hounds."

Charlotte sat down at the kitchen table and made some plans for what needed to be done, and when, so their guests would have the best possible experience. She took a moment to look around the beautiful kitchen and appreciate this place. She absolutely loved her role at the Inn, and she felt so blessed that she and Davis worked so well together. She really had a charmed life and was very happy.

Christmas music started playing in the living room.

"Everything's ready in here," Davis called to her.

Wonderful! He had gotten the dogs to lay down somewhere and it was time to decorate the tree. Charlotte left her list on the kitchen table and went to join him.

The tree was already lit up with thousands of small, white lights. Davis had straightened it so it looked much better than after the second time Bacardi had knocked it over. Every candle in the living room had been lit, making it look quite elegant. There was a fire burning in the fireplace, a perfect addition to the evening with the snow-covered landscape outside.

But Charlotte didn't really notice all of those other details, because her attention was on something else entirely.

Davis had not, in fact, gotten the dogs to go lay down.

Instead, they were sitting obediently in front of him facing her. Davis sat on the fireplace hearth with Bacardi on his right and Bean on his left. Each of the dogs had a sign hanging around their neck, and Davis held a sign up above their heads.

Davis' sign read 'Charlotte'.

Bacardi's sign read 'Marry'.

And Bean's sign read 'Me'.

"What?!" Charlotte exclaimed, covering her mouth with her hands.

Her excitement broke the dog's ability to be calm and they ran to her, signs flapping, and jumped around her feet, wanting to be part of whatever game she was enjoying.

"Wait, hang on," Davis said as he stood up and took out a tiny box that had been hidden inside the Christmas tree. He came to her and got on one knee. The dogs turned their attention to jumping on him.

"Get down, boys," Charlotte said with a laugh as she watched Davis try to get the ring box open and keep his balance at the same time.

"Charlotte," he managed to avoid being knocked over and still hold up the ring so she could see it sparkle in the Christmas lights. "I love you today more than ever. You have made my life complete," Bean started barking, unable to contain his joy at whatever was happening. Davis grinned, "You've made our lives complete. Will you be my wife?"

Charlotte nodded, too overcome with emotion to speak.

"That's a 'yes'?" He asked.

"Yes," she managed to say.

As he moved to take the ring out of its box, Bacardi lunged for it, thinking it was something wonderful for him. Bean hopped straight up and down and barked some more.

"Whoa, buddy!" Davis had to raise his arm high above his head to keep it away from the dog. For a moment, Charlotte thought either he was going to fall over or Bacardi was going to swallow the ring and ring box whole. But Davis kept his balance and got the dog to calm down with one arm while he held the ring safely in the air with his other arm. When it was safe, he took the ring out of the box and put it on her left ring finger.

"There, phew! That was close," he said and they both starting laughing.

Charlotte threw her arms around Davis' neck, thrilled to be engaged to the love of her life. Bacardi and Bean sensed the renewed excitement and went wild again. Davis pulled her down to him on the floor, then shielded her body with his as the dogs jumped joyfully around them. She ended up laying on her back on the rug, with Davis' body half over hers, protecting her from the happy chaos of their pups.

"This is it! The glamorous life of the Innkeeper's wife has begun!" Davis exclaimed.

Charlotte laughed again, then pulled him to her for a kiss. She wouldn't have it any other way.

Want more romance?
Find more titles by Darci Balogh at
knowheremedia.com/books

If you enjoyed this book, please consider leaving a review.

ABOUT THE AUTHOR

Darci Balogh is a writer and indie filmmaker from Denver. She grew up in the beautiful mountains of Colorado and has lived in several areas of the state over her lifetime. She currently resides in Denver where she raised her two glorious, intelligent daughters to functioning adulthood. This is, by far, one of her highest achievements.

She has a love-hate relationship with gardening, probably should dust more, adores dogs and is allergic to cats. She has been a writer since she was a child and enjoys crafting stories into novels and screenplays.

Big surprise, some of her favorite pastimes are reading and watching movies. Classic British TV is high on her 'Like' list, along with quietly depressing detective series and coffee with heavy cream.

Made in the USA
Middletown, DE
23 July 2020